THE WESTERN FRONTIER LIBRARY

THE TRUSTY KNAVES

UNIVERSITY OF OKLAHOMA PRESS : NORMAN

THE TRUSTY KNAVES

BY

Eugene Manlove Rhodes

WITH AN INTRODUCTION BY

W. H. Hutchinson

AND ILLUSTRATIONS BY

W. H. D. Koerner

The illustrations in this edition of *The Trusty Knaves* are by W. H. D. Koerner (1878–1938) and are reproduced here through the courtesy of Ruth Koerner Oliver.

International Standard Book Number: 0–8061–0975–0

Library of Congress Catalog Card Number: 76–160503

The Trusty Knaves is volume 49 in *The Western Frontier Library.*

CON RAZÓN

By W. H. Hutchinson

There are several reasons worth mentioning why this "Knavish book" holds a special place in the roster of Rhodesian writings. Among them is the fact that it brought Rhodes more money than any other of his stories: $7,500 from the *Saturday Evening Post*, where it appeared in three installments, April 18–May 2, 1931. This sum enabled him to pay his current burden of accumulated debts, which he incurred all of his life by a process of economic osmosis, and gave him the "road stake" necessary to move to La Jolla, California, for the final exile of his life. Parenthetically, it is worth noting that W. H. D. Koerner received $2,800 for the seven illustrations that enhanced the story's magazine appearance, while Rhodes' last *Satevepost* appearance —another three-parter, "Beyond the Desert" in 1934—brought him but $4,500 and Koerner but $2,100 for his seven illustrations. Not even the *Post* was Depression-proof.

This story also added a small tile to the mosaic of outlaws-on-horseback in the West-That-Was. Its appearance solved the mystery of where Bill Doolin had found sanctuary for some of the time between his breaking jail at Guthrie, Oklahoma, in January, 1896, and his death at the hands of Heck Thomas eight months later. That sanctuary had been at Rhodes' horse ranch high in the San Andrés Mountains, which separate New Mexico's White Sands from the *Jornada del Muerto* traversed by Juan de Oñate to colonize New Mexico for Spain.

Rhodes put Doolin into the story just as he remembered him.

I was the one the pony bucked on and Bill Doolin shot that horse to keep him from killing me, just as told in the yarn. Bill Doolin could not read or write, except his own name! I indicated as much when he dictated whenever he had to write, and signed by $ instead of scrawling his name. Perhaps I should have said so in as many words, but the man was my friend and I would not humiliate that friendly ghost.

He wrote again of Doolin to Alice Corbin Henderson, an associate of Harriet Monroe in the early years of *Poetry* and then living in Santa Fe.

To say truly, I have been revolving this story, in what I humorously refer to as my mind, for nearly thirty years. Here is Bill Doolin as he was, his freakish humor, his hardihood, his swift body, with a hint of the black hours of his melancholy fits—and I say of him as of "Erie" in the story

"What a Waste!" One thing I was forced to change. As five is to four—I have bettered his speech—as is 7 to 5. Because with backwoods phrases between hill-billy words and the technical phrases of cowland, it was not practical politix to be literal. The reader would find too much that he did not understand. As in the case of Lewis Mumford, he would need a good English version.

Doolin was not the only man outside the law who had used Rhodes' ranch as a hideout, or way station to elsewhere, and he and those like him gave substance to Rhodes' not entirely facetious feeling in later life that outlaws made better company than in-laws.

There is a zest and verve and swing to this story that sets it well apart from Rhodes' other work. Several of his short stories possess this *élan*, as do parts of many of his other novellas, but this is the only instance where he used "a rainbow for a skip rope" over such fictional distance. Perhaps this stems from the lack of feminine distractions in the story, thus enabling an unimpaired concentration upon the masculine characters of the masculine society of his youth. Perhaps it comes from the importunate intensity with which Rhodes confronted life and which he was able in this instance to give to all of the story characters. It may be due, as well, to the fact that he wrote this story in New Mexico, after twenty years of eastern exile, and the memory embers that had warmed him in New York were fanned into leaping, joyous flames as he re-lived and recalled those days when he and New Mexico were young—"There were no gods then and circles had no centers." There well may be another reason for this zestfulness.

For a dozen years before writing *The Trusty Knaves*, Rhodes had expended too much time and energy combatting the emerging literary trend towards "Psychobanalysis, Psex, Psherwood Anderson and the Conrad Aiken-void," which in his view held that "the chief end of man is his middle." His disgust at this "psexual perversion" became outraged ferocity at the concurrent depiction of everything in "these United, so to speak, States" as being indescribably rotten and capable of salvation only through subservience to some imported -ism.

In contrast to the gospel of Marxists and Fabians that it was necessary to create a new society, Rhodes felt that he and his kind were the latest, not the last, in a continuity of generations which already had made a new society and were improving it. He and those he had known and admired—sweating, toiling, striving men—always had been humanists enough to find joy in their daily survival tasks; hence he rejected out-of-hand the burgeoning view of such workers as part of "the masses" and thus exploited proletarians. "*A wife, a child, a brother, poverty and a country—what the Greeks had, I have,*" he once wrote.

Instead of deploring life's difficult struggle, Rhodes and the people of his youth and young manhood had embraced it. Neither he nor they had asked for more than the self-made luck of Aesop's frog drowning in a bowl of milk, which bestirred its limbs so vigorously that it churned up a pat of butter upon which to sit while pondering the next move. And when it came to any form of inexorable determinism, Rhodes expressed his feelings in a letter to the then *Saturday Review of Literature* which never saw the light of type.

That machinery is the royal road to ruin is a theory which has been stated by a thousand voices in chorus; the inter-bred chorus which chants the fashion of the hour. This theory about machinery is the touching and innocent confidence that fairy or fiend can alter the influence which causes bear upon results. It is what I do with the sword that is important. The sword can do nothing to me. If I use an aeroplane to smuggle heroin, that is not caused by any evil spell cast upon the wings; it is because I have the soul of a louse. If I drove an ox-cart, I would put it to the same use. If I bring terror and death to the road when I drive a car, it is not the plotting stars and my car that make me a murderer. It is because my heart is an anarch's heart, which flouts at regulations serving the general good. If I write drivel on the typewriter or drool it into a microphone, no malice of machinery contrived this imbecility. It is because I am an ass! If I wrote with a goose quill, I would still be an ass! One thing about machinery seems to have escaped notice: that it saves a lot of backache for the workers.

So, in writing *The Trusty Knaves*, Rhodes hymned his tribute to the people—the "ragged individualists"—and their values that had made his youth. To him, their rugged self-reliance embodied the heroic virtues—truth, honor, valor and communion with God, fortitude and magnanimity. It is this that gives the *élan vital* to what is regarded here as Rhodes' most sparkling tribute to the virtues of contributory democracy over a passion for participatory collectivism.

Chico State College
Chico, California

DEAR READER:

HERE are a few memories of yesterday's people. Was it really the day before? It does not seem so long.

Of all these people only three are alive today; Jack Farr, Lithpin Tham, Bob Martin, and myself. If that seems to be four people, let me add that both Bob Martin and myself went to the making of Johnny Pardee. I was the boy the bronc bucked on, and Bill Doolin shot that luckless horse, as described. Bob Martin, on the contrary, was foreman of the 7 T X at Engle, when he was twenty, just as Cole Railston was foreman of the Bar Cross at twenty-one. Two kid foremen: none better. Bob is my neighbor now, ninety miles away, and we get together on a sunny porch and tell sad stories of the death of kings. That smooth face of his is lined and furrowed now—just as Felipe's face, which once was worth the turning of any head to see, is now the battered face of the Sphinx.

Jack Farr is eighty-three—tall and straight still, but so thin and frail that he seems the ghost of a man. He has buckled up his belt another hole, so many times; his feet are slow, that were once so swift; his poor old nose is sharp and thin, like Cyrano's in one thing only, that it is the color of old ivory.—Do not pity him. His name was not Jack Farr, by the way. That was only what the name of the man was called. By the same token, Jack Farr, the real man in the flesh, was never a drinking man. It seemed kinder to use this one, to show what a pest a man can be to his friends, than to use a man who really drank. Nothing could be more unfriendly than a literal record of the words and deeds of a heavy drinker.

Bill Doolin was the first to go. When he told me good-bye, he rode straight to his death. That explains 'Taps' in the story. He did not say so—but I am sure he meant to bring his wife and child to the San Andres or the Jornada, and to start in new.

Pres Lewis was the hero of my boyhood. I have not yet found a better one. He had a Jovian serenity, in the most turbulent hours of that unquiet land, that I have never seen equaled. He will brighten up his corner of heaven.

Here is a good place to remember that a thousand and a thousand handsomely printed books have said —not casually, but shrieking and beating their breasts—that life in the Western half of the United

States has been all sodden misery, drab and coarse and low. These books also give very bad reports concerning another half of the United States—but I mention the West because, on examination, it appears that these writers knew nothing about the West except what they had learned by reading each other's books. You doubtless know these books. Americans are not Frenchmen, and it is just too bad. In all the West, through all a hundred years, these writers found nothing to love.

Plainly, if these books tell the truth, then any and all of my stories are shameless lies. And yet, and yet —here is what was once said of the early settlers of Illinois in a notable Life of Abraham Lincoln:

> Finding life hard, they helped each other with a general kindliness which is impracticable among the complexities of elaborate social organizations.

The defense rests. Once and for all, I hold that a barbarous society in which kindliness and helpfulness are spontaneous and inevitable was and is infinitely better than a civilization in which kindliness and helpfulness are impracticable. More than that, I sometimes wonder if our boasted 'high standard of living' is in any way different from the luxury which destroyed Persia and Rome.

What I remember is generosity, laughter, courage, and kindness. Kindness most of all; kindness from evil men and worthless men, as well as from good men. Therefore this humble star is dear. And I have never had reason to believe that this our world is greatly loved by the highly civilized.

After all, I claim but little for the people of my stories. And as a sort of preface to this story, and to all my stories, I must tell you something about Beppo.

He was a kitten, a black kitten with enormous yellow eyes. His mother was poisoned when he was very small and we fed him with a medicine-dropper for many days. It was touch and go to save him. A thin, tottering, pitiful kitten when he first managed to scramble up my stuffed chair to my shoulder, to sing his first little triumph song and to lick my ear as all he could do then for his share of the kindly bargain.

A plump kitten then, a big-eyed kitten with free choice of two laps to sleep on, a marvelous rubber ball that was all his own, a garden full of flowers expressly for his sniffing tours; proud and happy when he was allowed to walk with the two old people who were all the family he knew and all the world he knew. It is charged that cats hold themselves aloof. Beppo never did. He accepted us as equals and was never once unkind.

A jaunty cat, a swaggering cat, a cat who exacted his rights: a cat who, when he wanted in or out, asked once to have the door opened, and then promptly did his endeavor to tear the wire screen out by main force. When he was about six months old, we got another black kitten, just weaning age, for companion and playmate. That was Damocles, who sits beside me as I write these lines.

Those were the great days! Wild racings and chasings, scampering and climbing—and such a delightful sniffing of every flower, the first thing in the morning! Such wrestlings and fight-teachings! And with this last came problems. Damocles was such a little cat. Before our eyes, Beppo sat him down to consider; before our eyes, even while we watched him, he evolved and perfected a code of ethics. It was, for all intents and purposes, identical with the best codes men have made for themselves, and there was no article of it which could have originated in any heart but a gentleman's. But there was this difference: Beppo did not break his code.

Damocles was such a little, little cat—sadly tumbled and wooled about by big Beppo, twice his weight. But he must be taught the essential virtues of cathood, courage and self-defense and the art to fight. Therefore, small squeakings of dismay went all unheeded. But there was sanctuary—a rattan-bound stool. When Damocles took to the stool, Beppo would put up a tentative paw. If Damocles struck out at it, those gleeful rompings went on. But if the challenge was not accepted, then that was the end of the bout. The little cat was tired, or perhaps the little cat was bruised: Beppo sighed audibly and subsided. Not once was sanctuary violated.

Again, the little cat was allowed handicap for size. The top of the great stuffed chair was reserved for him; from that vantage to repel Beppo's furious attacks from the floor. Again, Beppo lay on his back under the rattan stool and the little cat stood on the stool; with this handicap, they waged desperate battle.

When the little cat was asleep, it was no fair to molest him, not even to arouse him: Beppo stalked stiff-legged, with blazing eyes and bristling mustache, impatient. But it was not allowed to awaken Damocles. Little cats must have their sleep out.

Milk was for little cats. When milk was in the saucer, Beppo waited complacently until Damocles had his fill. But meat was different. That was primarily for big cats and Beppo sailed in at once.

They never were angry with each other and never jealous. Damocles pre-empted a tall stool, table-high, and perched upon it to assist at our meals. Beppo watched him admiringly, ungrudgingly, from the floor. Not once did he attempt to poach on the little cat's preserves. We provided a shorter stool for Beppo, after a little. He accepted it gratefully enough, and they sat side by side to assist—but there was never any confusion about the stools. The tall stool was the discoverer's own.

The great event of the day was when the two cats walked abroad with me; and they were wild with pride and delight the first time the lady of the house made a fourth. Hi, that was a merry time! Such scurryings, such runnings ahead, hidings in a bush, and pouncings out upon a terrified family!

There was the same ending for each happy day. Every night, at ten o'clock, no more and no less, Beppo eyed Damocles severely, pounced upon him, held him exactly as Punch held his club, and proceeded to make the little cat's toilet. Strugglings, wailings, were of no avail. Eyes ablaze, Beppo turned the little cat over and over and gave him a good washing. And so to bed, a tangle of black legs.

They had a thousand jolly games of their own devising. Strangest was the irrigation game, in warm weather: to sit side by side with their backs to the rising water, both black tails extended at full length, trying which could longest endure the shiversome touch of climbing water. A twitch or a quiver counted the same as flight itself. It was a weird watching to see them.

You must know of a sad blemish on Beppo's fame. He was afraid of dogs. Not reasonably afraid, prudently afraid. Dogs filled him with abject terror. It dated back to a luckless hour of his puniest kittenhood. There was a neighbor dog, a hundred miles away. He was a Scotty named Jockson Beetle, a very fine dog, but a terror to all cats to whom he had not been properly introduced. Jockson Beetle came visiting, bringing his family with him, his two kind and loving gods—and neither Jockson Beetle nor his family knew there was any Beppo cat. We rushed out on the lawn to eager greetings—and Jockson Beetle went up on the covered porch where poor Beppo lay asleep. Jockson Beetle saw and charged furiously—and that would have been all, except that the poor, frantic kitten performed a miracle of flight along a bare concrete wall. He never got over that fright.

This was long before Damocles came. And it chanced that when Beppo was almost grown, our next-door neighbor (half a block of vacant lots intervening) had a general cleaning up of a storeroom behind the garage and put out six or eight delightful boxes of souvenirs for the garbage-man.

Beppo and Damocles promptly went on a tour of inspection. As it happened, I was watching them as they wrestled together in the lee of the boxes.

Now there lived next door a frolicsome puppy, young Floppit, a black bird dog. His family, I believe, knew him by another name. But his mode of progression was by a series of sidewise leaps and bounds, so I have never been able to remember him other than as Floppit. As I watched, Floppit came bouncing around the boxes. Simultaneously, a long black streak came down the walk. That was Beppo.

He came to the corner of his own home lot, and turned, every hair a-bristle. The puppy was bounding about, yelping. Damocles had not moved. He had not even fluffed his tail. He regarded young Floppit's antics with puzzled interest, but it had not occurred to him to be scared. Beppo gave one despairing and frantic wail of warning. Damocles did not come. So Beppo went back—this most imperfect gentle knight! True, he did not go back as fast as he came, but he went fast and he did not falter—back to what he dreaded most on earth. Sans Peur is admirable, doubtless—but this was Greatheart. I have no brighter memory from my days.

Be patient: this joyful story is all too brief. As he grew to maturity, Beppo went in for society. His engagements kept him away for days at a time, sometimes for a week, and he came back all tattered and torn. This caused his family much uneasiness. A rough and uninhabited promontory runs out into the sea just beyond us, and we had heard coyotes there. But Beppo came and went, and our fears subsided. In the fullness of time, Damocles, in turn, made tentative excursions. On his second adventure, Beppo was at home, much the worse from his wars, and very uneasy about Damocles. He sat on the window-sill, watching. The lady of the house saw me coming a block away, carrying truant Damocles. Beppo saw us at the same time, she says; pricked up his ears, hopped down, and went to the front door to greet his pardner. This was about four in the afternoon. They had a great visit together for three hours or so. At early twilight Beppo came to me, firmly demanding that I should let him out. I opened the door and he said thank you, as he always did; he strolled down the path with his arrogant tail aflaunt, turned at the sidewalk, flicked his big eyes at me as he turned. I like to remember that it was a friendly look. He sauntered down to the sea: and met there the Terminator of Delights and the Separator of Companions.

Well! I claim for these men of whom I write no greater equipment than Beppo's, and no other: a joyous and a loving heart, a decent respect for others and for himself, and courage enough to master fear. No more than that: and what I tell you of these unforgotten friends is true telling and no lie. Not the detailed adventures, but the arms that mocked at weariness, the feet that trod on fear.

EUGENE MANLOVE RHODES

THE TRUSTY KNAVES

CHAPTER I

A SMALL and scattered herd grazed over the False Divide between Plomo and Horsethief, and turned down into Gridiron; something around six hundred head of cattle. They were thin and weak, gaunted for water. A little bunch of saddle ponies, with a few extra work horses, grazed apart, well to one side of the wagon road for the sake of better grass, and a few hundred yards ahead of the cattle; with a similar interval, a small band of white Angoras flanked them, with a small boy for viceroy. The herders were five: George Carmody, square-faced and grizzled—Old George, although he was barely more than forty—three children, Judge, Jim and Jenny, stepladdered from Judge's eighteen down to Jenny's twelve; and Charlie Bird. Charlie had been wagon boss when the B 4 brand was great. Dogged and faithful, he followed its fallen fortunes. Drought was upon the land, the price of cattle had fallen from thirty dollars to twelve, still falling. The B 4 was struggling westward for rumored grass of Arizona.

Jenny was the horse wrangler; small Jimmy, on the small Ginger pony, drove the goats. A mile ahead, four horses drew the canvas-covered chuck wagon, and Lee Carmody sat in the shade of the tilt to drive. It may be said here that the five dusty herders were cheerful herders as well, and that Lee Carmody's face was as comely and pleasant as it was when Old George was Young George, and she was Young George's young wife. It was one of our folk-ways to take good and bad as they come, with little boasting and with no complaint.

High in the north, close above them, a sharp black ridge made a fin on the crest of False Divide. At the scarp of this ridge a horse and his rider stood motionless, outlined against the sky, looking down upon the weary herd. The rider leaned forward, both hands on the saddle horn. A scanty wind beat back the broad brim of a hat already tip-tilted to heaven and clinging precariously to his head. The stronger cattle in the lead began to string out, moving faster. Seeing this, the horse herd moved on to check them. The observer lifted his reins, and his horse picked his downward way gingerly through the broken lava of the ridge. Man and horse turned into the dust behind the plodding drag. George Carmody angled across to meet them.

The newcomer was tall, noticeably slender, something under middle age. His face was long, thin, quiet, freckled so darkly that each freckle stood out, embossed against that tanned and leathern face. Thick, unruly hair, blown back against that tiptilt hat, was darkest red, all but black. His nose was long and straight and thin, with a hooked tip. A brindled mustache was ragged above an uncurving thin-lipped mouth; wide-set pale blue eyes were watchful, but friendly. He raised an open palm in salute.

'Howdy, stranger! Guess them lead cattle smell water, don't they? I see 'em stringin' out.'

'Yes.' The tall man fell in beside Carmody. 'Windmill in the draw, beyond that next little rise. Two mile or so.'

'Your place?'

The tall man shook his head. 'Patterson's place. Ladder Line Camp. Got most a dozen wells and still reaching out. Controls pretty much all this end of our peaceful valley, Erie does. Gives the Railroad brand—like this.' He traced the Railroad brand with a finger on his horse's neck. 'Only we call it the Ladder, mostly. Me, I'm way west and south, beyond the railroad. Over on the Gavilan.' His eyes rose to a far-off jumble of splintered hills; he pointed with a blunt chin, Indian fashion; pursing his lips, again in Indian fashion. 'Name of Farr.'

W. H. D
Koerner

said Carmody gravely. 'For money is just what I haven't got. Down on the river I loaded up the chuck wagon, and it took my last dollar.'

'Well, that's my orders,' said Garst, 'and I got no leeway. It's a new one on me, too, and I don't get any particular pleasure out of it. If I stretch the price, can't you turn over a couple of yearlings, or something?'

Carmody's face hardened. 'You look like a cowman and you ought to know better than that. No other brand goes on B 4 cattle. No man on any range has any right to any cowbrute branded B 4. I sell no cow stuff, except to ship back to the States. I'll have to pay you with a pony, I reckon—and God knows I've none to spare. If I had anything fat enough for beef, now ——'

A sharp, barking laugh, checked abruptly. That was Farr. Albert Garst whirled upon him.

'Can't you keep your long nose out of this?' he snarled.

'Why, Albert, can't a body laugh?' said Farr soothingly. 'I was just thinking of all the fat stuff about here—yours and everybody's.' His eyes widened a trifle and regarded the red-faced Garst with close attention. Not a stare, or a threatening look—steady and thoughtful contemplation. He put both hands on the saddle horn and leaned forward. 'This is all foolishness, Bert, and you know it. We'll water these thirsty cattle now, and see about maybe paying some way when we get around to it. Let down the bars, Carmody.'

'You just think so!' Albert made one quick step, his hand shot out and reached behind the gatepost. A double-barreled shotgun leaped to his shoulder, the hammer clicked, the muzzle jerked in to rake Farr at the waistband. 'Now, you long, lean, red-muzzled son of Satan, if you move one finger towards your gun I'll blow you in two!'

Farr's contemplative eyes held unchanged, motionless. 'Albert,' said Farr, in a soft drawl which ended in a rising note, 'what kind of shot have you got in them cartridges?'

'Buckshot, you old hyena! Buckshot at ten feet!'

'Then,' said Farr gently, 'we'll have to settle it some other way. I'll tell you what, my boy. I'll give you my note. Pay it tomorrow in Target.'

'Note, me eye! You'll give me a check.'

'Sure enough! I just can't get used to that new bank of ours. Always forgetting it. . . . All right, Albert; you win. Let the hammer down. I won't shoot.' Moving those attentive eyes at last, he glanced down at his unbuttoned vest and fished out a new check book and a new pencil. He made ready to write, using his saddle horn for table.

'I want you both to understand that I have no gun on me,' said Carmody; his voice was hard. 'It is not my habit to let another man do my fighting for me, or pay for me.'

'Eh? Oh, that's all right,' said Farr. 'Sure, I knew you had no gun. And you can pay me back when you get good and ready.'

'Well, sir, I'm obliged to you, sir—I am so. I'll remember this.'

'Oh, that's all right. You can do somebody a turn sometime. . . . Nice fat cattle you got, Albert. . . . Pay to the order of Erie Patterson, thirty dollars.'

'Make that thirty-five,' said Albert. 'Forty or fifty head of horses and a bunch of goats.'

Farr raised his head and his disconcerting eyes were again unwinking and motionless. 'Thirty dollars. Your damned old gun might miss fire.' He signed his name and tore out the check.

Albert leaned his shotgun against the fence and took down the bars. The B 4 wagon came around a curve in the twisting draw, the saddle horses close behind.

'Have your wagon drive around the tank, Mr. Carmody,' said Albert. 'You'll find a faucet and a hose there to fill your barrel with.'

The horse herd passed through the gate and made for the troughs. Farr had ridden aside to get out of the dust. He came back now and leaned on the saddle horn again. 'Albert,' he said, and his drawl was slower than ever, 'would you mind letting me see one of those cartridges?'

'Oh, my Lord! I thought you was gone. You'll keep on fooling around till somebody gets hurt.'

'Why, Albert, I ain't in no fix to hurt nobody. The'retically, I'm done dead. You had me, if you was a mind to pull the trigger. So I'm in no mind to shoot you. Our gunning is all done, now and ever after, so far as I'm concerned. I just wanted to know if that was sure-enough buckshot in them cartridges.'

'I told you so, didn't I? Are you calling me a liar?'

'Now, now,' said Farr, 'I just almost know you wouldn't lie—not of a Wednesday. But I'd kinder like to see.'

'I think,' said Albert, 'that you are absolutely the most aggravating, cantankerous old idiot in the whole round world.'

He took the shotgun, hesitated perceptibly, broke it, slipped out one of the cartridges and tossed it up to the horseman. 'There, you old fool! Are you satisfied now?'

Farr caught the cartridge, dug out wadding with his knife, and dropped eight buckshot into his cupped palm. He nodded. 'All right, Albert. No grudge. No feud. But if you had deceived me and stuck me up with a mess of bird shot, I shouldn't have liked it one mite. I could take a mess of bird shot and then plug you, I judge.' He paused for rumination. 'I'll tell you what, Albert. No gun grudge, but why couldn't we arrange a little fist feud for a follow-up? Sometime when we're not busy?'

'Any time you say, and no time like right this very now. Hop down off that horse and I'll break you in two!'

Farr considered this proposition and shook his head regretfully. 'I aim to be right busy, next three or four days, finding out what Erie Patterson means by charging for water. When did anybody ever hear of such doings as that? Thirty dollars ain't no more to him than five cents. This calls for my able mind. I can 'tend to you later. Any time you see me comin', and me with no gun on me, you set out the liniment and bandages handy. I'll bring some arniky along.' He paused for meditations which seemed to be pleasant, for his straight mouth curved to a smile. 'So you think you can break me in two, do you?'

'I know I can!'

'Mebbe so, mebbe so. I'll tell you what—I'll

make you a little bet on that. I like you, Albert, and I sort of hate to see you working for this Railroad brand. So we'll fix it like this: If I lick you good and plenty—lay you out cold—then you'll come over and work for me.'

'And if I have to carry you to bed, what do I get out of it?'

'If you do that I'll be dead and you'll be leaving here in a hurry. So you stand to win either way. . . . I'll bring the buckboard. We won't either one of us feel like riding a horse.'

CHAPTER II

It was a queer country. There were days when the circling mountains were near and clear, sharp and shining, where a thousand facets threw back the sun, every dimple and wrinkle showing plain, each gorge and cleft black and beckoning; when every wandering ridge and ground swell of the great plain was cameo-clear, and you were a brisk, upstanding man who rode, prancing and mettlesome, on affairs of weight and consequence; a sprightly person, interesting to yourself and to others.

But this was not one of those days. When Farr was an hour on the short cut from Line Camp to Target, the air fell hot and still, the far-off ranges made an unangled, wavering blur, blue beyond a trembling, sun-shot haze of dancing dust motes. The ridged and rolling plain was sea-flat now, smudged, undimensioned, vague and dim; and Elmer Farr saw himself a meaningless midge, creeping unnoticed beneath a brazen sky. This salutary frame of mind was dispelled when he topped a rise and saw below him the long loops of

Corkscrew Draw, and a horse climbing to him on a zigzag trail—Johnny Pardee on his Strawberry horse. Farr drew rein and waited.

The trail was sharp and stiff. The last scramble climbed a staircase ledge of limestone. Strawberry puffed noisily, his nostrils dilating. Brown Jug held his head high, gazing beyond the canyon deeps with a lofty expression which implied that Strawberry was disgracefully fat, and also gave a distinct impression that Jug had both hands in his pockets, head up and chest out. Which was absurd, because Jug was Farr's horse and had no pockets. Strawberry snorted and laid his ears back. Johnny slid off.

'Slim, you got any water in that canteen?'

'Sure have.'

'Gimme,' said Johnny. As he drank, Farr climbed stiffly from his horse and sat on the ledge with his feet hanging over. To him, there, came Johnny with the canteen—a young and smaller man, with a sparkling face, unlined and smooth. That boyish face was deceptive. This was a man proved and trusted. At twenty-two, Johnny was foreman of the Packsaddle outfit, with men of twice his age, tough and seasoned—men of name and standing in the cow country—glad to be one of that hard and choosy bunch. He sat cross-legged beside Farr and rolled himself a smoke.

'Johnny,' said Farr dreamily, 'did you ever see any of this here driven snow?'

'All I know about snow is that I wish I had some to put in this canteen. Anything gnawing on you, old-timer? If you feel a sort of unusual sensation creeping around just above and back of your eyes, why, that might be an idea, you know. Driven snow, you said? Yes, yes; go on!'

'Once I was pure, like that,' said Farr. 'But it was a long while ago. I have done so much meanness myself, that my mind has soured on me. I'm not simple and trustful like I was. No, sir; I'm given to low suspicions, and I got one coming on right now.'

'Tell it to me.'

'Fork that fat plug of yours, then, and side me to Target. Tell you as we go.'

'I was sort of wishful to drop in on Albert.'

'Now, now; nothing to do till the round-up begins. You saunter along with me and Jug, and I'll tell you the sad story of my life.'

'Poor Albert, he had no liking for that job—none whatever,' said Farr in conclusion of the sad story. 'He was all het up. I had me nearly two hours to study on it and I've made all the guesses there is. Me and Jug have just about got it ciphered out. Erie Patterson, he knew all about this Carmody a-coming, and him out of money. He done instructed

Albert to get Carmody riled up, so he'd yank his old forty-come-odd and throw down on Albert and water his bossy cows by main force.'

'Huh! Damn likely—and Albert to maybe get himself shot some?'

'Yes, sir. Just like that. That's why Albert didn't like it. That's how come that shotgun leaning against the gatepost—just in case. Loaded with buckshot. Buckshot in the middle of this plain, with nothing bigger'n a quail between here and the hills? This play is the only way to make any sense of that buckshot. Albert was willing to be stuck up, but he didn't yearn to be actually killed, if it really came to shooting. And when I put in—well, I've deviled Albert right smart, off and on, and he is just a little leery of me. He jumped up to see what he hung by.'

'But why? Why pull off a risky stunt like that?'

'Why egg Carmody on to make a gun play? Simple. Then they jerk him to jail, law him to a frazzle, and buy his little bunch of cattle at half price.'

'Why, Jack! How you do talk!'

'It's the only way that makes any sense. No one would take such a chance for just thirty dollars. They aim to annex those cattle. . . . What's that? Who's they? Erie Patterson for one—and whoever we catch at it. It doesn't follow that Albert was in on that part. Probably wasn't. Albert is sort of fair to middlin'. Patterson just about told him to charge for watering that herd, but not to use no gun to collect with. Albert's pure and innocent face told me he was studyin' about why. And he didn't half like it.'

'But Erie is out of cash,' objected Johnny, 'spreadin' himself all over the shop, and he's borrowed from our new, shiny bank up to his neck. You know that. You're one of the straw bosses in the bank and you passed on his notes. Erie's got no money to buy more cattle with.'

'Just so. Therefore, there's someone else in on the deal. That's the point. Have you maybe noticed of late any queer goings-on in this happy valley of ours?'

'I have so. Leaving to one side the normal amount of clerical errors in the branding business. Granger takes up a homestead for himself on the Temporal. His house burns down. Another long lad settles at Carizo, and his house burns up. Freight cars looted on the Target side tracks. More freight cars robbed at the same place. Ore stolen from freight wagons in Target. Drunks rolled at Target. Reemarkable hands held at Jim's Gem against prosperous visitors from the East. Mines salted for prosperous visitors. And so on down the line.'

'Johnny,' said Farr, 'I do believe they have been doing it on purpose.'

'You mean a gang?'

'Just that. A nice new jail and it full all the time, but never a man for anything really low-down and ornery—drunk and disorderly; disturbing the peace; toting deadly weapons—the like of that. Jail till they rustle money for a big fine. Profiting thereby—town marshal, sheriff, Hissoner Francis Truesdale Humphries, J. P., and lawyers. Not one of 'em turning a hand at anything really useful; and catching not one of the skunks that have been doing the dirty work.'

'So you think law and lawbreakers——'

'Partners. You said it. Then, thinks I, why not get about six or some reliable rascals together and look-see? So I thought of you right off—and here you're the first man I meet. A leading, I calls it.'

'Well, where do you propose to start to untangle?'

'Done started. Erie Patterson, railroader—takes his name from a railroad; calls his brand the Railroad. Ex-conductor on the T.C. Made his start dividing cash fares with the company. You know that?'

'Oh, *si!* Tossed the money up to the ceiling.

What didn't come down went to the company. Go on.'

'So Patterson quits the T.C. and goes in for cattle. You and me and most, we call his brand the Ladder, but Erie himself, he always calls it the Railroad brand. Some several old railroaders working for him. Dave Salt for one. Railroad bull—don't know a cow from a caboose. Killer, I guess. Well! Next point. Young fella me lad, can you go down to them locked cars on the siding and pick out one loaded with wagons? Or windmills? Or saddles? Or general merchandise? No, says you. Well, someone picked out just what they wanted. Never a car broken into at Target yet but it was loaded with something mighty handy to use around here. No pianos or farming implements ever bothered yet. Well?'

'Inside information?'

'Nothing else. And then? As to the Carmody case? The next step?'

'Humph! Cattle ranches, railroaders, law, somebody with money enough to buy that herd ——'

'What's the matter with Kames? He's a lawyer.'

'And was once a lawyer for the T.C. in a small way; till they fired him. Why? Not for lack of brains. He's a slick one—Kames. But I must stick to the Carmody case. . . . Says dear old Elmer to me, sezzee: What's the next move?' Johnny reflected, and spoke slowly, handling words as a man handles his feet when he walks a rope: 'The man is broke. And I want to get him in bad and buy him in at forced sale. Oh, *si!* . . . And I tried to force him into a ranikiboo play at Line Camp. Well? So I could set John Law on him? Oh, *si!* And Carmody can't go through Gridiron Flat without watering at Target. And the T.C. Railroad pipes the Target water from the hills. Why, the next play is to have the agent charge him for watering at the stock pens.'

'Correct. Let's ride!'

'But, Slim, the T.C. will never stand for that. Their play is to boost the cattle business.'

'What does the T.C. know about what goes on here? If the earth opened and swallowed Target, San Francisco wouldn't know it till steer-shipping time. That yellow-bellied station agent could do it on his own. Let's you and me sort of permeate around and begin to Stop, Look and Listen. And,' said Slim Jack Elmer Farr, 'we want to gather in some re-enforcements. This will be a nifty job and us two are not enough.'

'So far,' said Johnny Pardee, 'this has been mighty small potatoes for a gang, if there is a gang. Picayunish, petty larceny. Piking.'

'Maybe they're just getting started,' Farr suggested. 'Feeling their way. Trying out candidates. But they stole enough from the railroad already to outfit a man-sized general-merchandise store, and if they aim to grab a whole brand of cattle this crack, that ain't exactly hen-roost stuff. That ain't all, either. Them nesters that got burned out by act of God, they were single men. The drunks, they was grown up. And nobody ever grieved themselves into the grave on account of pilfering from a railroad, or any kind of company or corporation, or the good old Government. But this Carmody guy, he's got a woman and three kids. That's different. 'Tain't just like rolling a drunk or robbing a train, or an express company, or —— Why, Johnny! Johnny Pardee!' Farr reined in his horse. His eyes narrowed, his lips slightly parted, wrinkles ridged his dusty brow, he held his head sidewise, as if he listened to something far-off and faint.

'Slim Jack,' said Johnny Pardee, 'come out of it! "I would not chide thee, Marguerite, nor mar one joy of thine so sweet"—but you've not been hitting it up again, have you? Excuse me for mentioning it, but you do, you know, when the sign is just right. Why, you old fool, you're plumb agitated. What's eating you now?'

'Johnny,' said the old fool, drawling, 'I've been

pretty lenient in my judgments about robbing trains and banks, and so on. Boys will be boys, and all that sort of thing. Banks back in Missouri and Illinois, you know. But this little bank here—why, that bank is yours and mine and everybody's! If anything was to happen to that bank, I'd be real peevish. I would so. I seem to see the whole subject in a new light, sort of. Miners, storekeepers, cowmen, everybody roundabout, all the way from Argentine to the border, they got a little money tucked away in there. Not such a gosh-awful lot, all told, but so long as it was scattered about, it would 'a' needed a lot of exertion to have made way with that money. Now we got it all bunched up for 'em, handy as a pocket in a shirt.'

'Roll over. You're having a nightmare. Mr. Cleveland done wrote and cautioned us to humor you all we could. But this is too much.'

'Listen, infant! Who was the prime mover in getting up this bank? I ask you. Ellis Kames, lawyer. Now what does Ellis Kames do? His open-and-aboveboard business? Livin' on the unlucky.'

Johnny interrupted: 'Also, sharing the spoil with the strong arm of the law. Who is the strong arm? Jim Yewell, town marshal; Steve Davis, sheriff; and the justice of the peace. Did any one of the four of them ever earn one round hard dollar by actual producing? The answer is: Not since they hit Gridiron. They are just like ticks in a cow's ear. Lilies of the field. The question now is: If I was sheriff, and if I then robbed a bank, and if I was then equipped with warrant and handcuffs, and went out looking for myself—would I ever catch myself?'

'Who's loony now?' said Slim Jack Elmer Farr.

The two friends reached Target soon after sunset, but it was ten o'clock when Farr tapped at the door of the telegraph office. Paul Nichols, the night operator, had barely time to close the door when the sounder stammered and choked.

Paul waved his hand. 'Newspapers. Help yourself,' he said as he slid into a chair and snatched up a pencil.

The sounder stuttered and spluttered and then settled to a snare-drum rataplan of train orders, while the flying pencil took them down. After which, young Paul pushed back his chair and turned a cheerful face on his guest. 'Well, old Rain-in-the-Face, what's on your chest?'

'I hardly know how to set about this,' said Farr. 'Are you scary, or dishonest, or part human? Do I bully you, bribe you, or just take a chance that you're decent?'

Paul laughed. 'Far be it from me to set up any

fixed rules. You just try whichever way you think will get the best results. I gather,' said Paul, 'that you want me to do something. Probably something that I shouldn't hadn't oughtn't.'

'No such thing. If you come projecting out to my ranch and asked me what hosses would work, I'd tell you. Whereas and aforesaid, to wit, namely, ss., I don't know as much about railroads as you do about horses. You tell me. Prick up your ears and listen to my tale of woe.' So saying, he gave the bare outlines of the sale of water to the B 4 herd, but said no word of shotgun or suspicions. 'New stuff, that is. I've seen water sold before, but that was where a man went off in the big middle of a desert and dug him a well for that purpose. In that case, he earned his money. But here, with plenty wells, shallow water—one stockman charging another—it's a low-down outrage. Dirty work at the crossroads. Now look! Erie Patterson and Mr. Wade Barton, station agent and your esteemed chief, are thick as thieves in a mill. What I look for is for Patterson to set Barton up to charge our wandering cowman for watering here in Target shipping pens. What I aim to do is to stop that short, never to go again. My idea is to wire one big howl and one promise true that if the T.C. pulls that stuff, I will henceforth and forever, amen, with all my friends, if any, drive my steers over and ship 'em on the Santa Fé. Signed, Elmer Farr. How about it? Where do I wire to who to tell him why.'

'My dear old fossil,' said Paul, 'your unworthy surmise proves you to be yourself no better than an evil-hearted rogue. Speaking as your lifelong friend of the last three days, I would advise you,' said Paul, 'to tuck in your shirt and otherwise readjust your attire.'

'My fair child,' said Farr, 'it is just because of that evil heart you speak of that I know exactly what another low-lifed scoundrel will do under a given set of circumstances. This being thus, we will now proceed. Tell it to me!'

'A railroad doesn't care any more about freight than you do about your left eye,' said the operator. 'The man you want is the general freight agent. You know what will happen if you send that wire, I suppose?'

'Barton will be kicked out, heels over head.'

'Not by a jugful. Someone will listen in and tip Barton off. He will then make no mention of any charge for water. If anybody is wishing trouble on your Texas outfit, they'll try something else. You'll be out the price of one night message, and the T.C. will mark opposite your name "Buttinsky, Trouble-Maker." '

'Right as rain,' said the cowman. 'You write me

off the name and address of the big head devil in the main office. I'll fix up my telegram and make it stiff. If Mr. Agent doesn't make any charge for watering that herd, you are hereby authorized to kick me good and hard at high noon on the Plaza. But if he tries to spring his holdup on Brother Carmody, I give him my telegram to send.'

'He'll back down,' said Paul.

'Sure he will. And right afterward, when I get around to it, he'll lose his job for grafting.'

Paul leaned back in his chair, rolled his eyes to the ceiling, made a church with his finger tips, and coughed delicately. 'You mentioned a bribe, I believe?' he suggested.

Farr rose and made for the door.

'You speak too late, brother. I've got what I want and I have no more use for you.' He slammed the door behind him and went whistling down the hall.

CHAPTER III

GRIDIRON FLAT was high and hot. It lay exactly where the backbone of the continent should have been. Events had happened here, leaving mountains scattered and tossed like jackstraws of a baby god. They made a broken circle about Gridiron; a boundary, but not a wall. The shining ranges lay criss-cross, cater-cornered, end on, every way except wallwise—tower, saw tooth, ax edge, spearhead, cone, pyramid. In the north, dominant, giving the flat a name, stood the prodigious bulk of San Lorenzo. From granite reaches of those far-off hills, water was piped to Target—pure water, which would not cake in boiler tubes. Following the compass points were Staircase, Plomo, Horsethief, Moncayo, Breen's, Gavilan, Argentine, with a pass for every comma. The Trans-Continental was a young and hasty railroad then, and a branch line to the silver town of Argentine climbed through Silver Gap, between San Lorenzo and Argentine Peak. Anyone who now cares for a little railroad of his own might today do well to apply to the T.C. for the Argentine Spur. The T.C. will pay for the deed and give you a bonus.

Gridiron was not really flat. It looked that way, but when you crossed it, you found it to be a deep saucer. Pusher engines from Target led a dog's life helping trains up Heartbreak Hill on the west, and eastward to Misery on the False Divide. Nor was that all. Target, the metropolis, perched midway of the plain in the center of an S-shaped boss. The T.C., young and hasty, as aforesaid, had built a straightaway from Misery to Heartbreak, and thereby crossed that S ridge three times. Pres Lewis, freighting ore down from Staircase, spoke of this fact to his wheelers, as the freight train bobbed up and down before them, and smiled indulgently, as if the T.C. were a favorite child of his.

Despite the high mountains roundabout, this low and crooked ridge was reputed to be the true watershed. Legend told that the run-off of the rainy season found its way northward to the Californian Gulf, westward to the Mexican Gulf. It seemed improbable. There was no visible outlet; whichever way you looked was uphill. Moreover, the seas mentioned did not lie in the directions mentioned, and it never rained, anyhow. Target shrugged at that drainage system as an innocent myth, like Santa Claus, or that stork story. Who cared, anyhow?

Gridiron was grassy, bare, bushy, treeless, cedared, flinty, sandy, dusty, hard, stony, gravelly, gray, white, brown and red—everything except muddy and green. And from every pass not served by the T.C., wagon roads came to Target like spokes to a hub. Imports—postage stamps, playing cards and schoolma'ams. Exports—beef, wool and silver. They ship no silver from Target now.

That was what Pres Lewis was freighting—silver concentrates, sacked for shipment to the smelter. That mile of thin red sand had been heavy going, and as the wagons rolled out to hard road again, the steaming horses stopped unbidden, to rest and puff before they tackled the last grade into Target. Such was the custom. Pres swung down from the saddle for the better resting of Punch, the wheeler. Punch eyed him comfortably. Beyond question, Punch was wondering if they would load out in the morning, or lay over two nights in Target, as sometimes happened.

Lindauer Place was the heart of Target, the oldest building, and the best. It fronted the Plaza, one massive block from street to street; one story high, but such a story! To begin with, the stone foundations rose three feet above ground. For the floor was level with the porch and the porch was wagon high. Lindauer had a solid mind, and these solid walls were to serve his children's children. Three-foot adobe, they rose fifteen feet to the ceiling. Then the flat roof; then the high parapet, sure defense against arrow and bullet, which had once been a very fort in war, but was now only a habit. Three and fifteen and one and four, making twenty-three feet high for one story of service.

Later advices report that a new device has replaced the wagon, and that it has been needful to raise the street level before Lindauer Place so that long porch may be running-board high. The plans we make! It was the successors of Herman Lindauer who filled in that street with concrete. Lindauer's sons are in California now, planning wisely for their sons.

Lindauer's General Store sprawled along the east end of the block. There were no catalogues. You asked for what you wanted and it was handed over the counter. Holland House, the best and only hotel of Target, fronted west and north on the other corner. Sandwiched between was Jim's Gem, saloon and house of chance, long and narrow, lamplit by night and by day. A door opening from the hotel lobby to the bar, a door direct from Lindauer's, explained why this dark and narrow site was desirable.

Two features are yet untold of the Lindauer Block. In the great open spaces of the Lindauer Store, newly partitioned in brick, a small corner fronted the Plaza in plate glass, overlooked East Street through high new windows, magnificent with new iron grilles, ornate and twisted; and in front a new sign was blue and gold and glorious:

THE FIRST BANK OF TARGET

The other feature was that the wagon-high platform of thick planks was roofed over to make a shaded porch before hotel, saloon and store—a porch fourteen feet wide and a block long, a porch with iron hitching rings for horse or team, with benches, tables and chairs for the uses of men; a porch which was to be danced on in a later year; a porch which was lobby, assembly room and senate hall for Target and for Gridiron. And John Cecil Calvert sat tip-tilt on that porch, forty years ago.

John Cecil Calvert was one-and-twenty, fresh from Ann Arbor. This was his second day in Target. His eyes drank in the splendor of a sun-drenched world, his mind revolved the curious and interesting information he had obtained, by dint of eager questioning, during the crowded hours of those two days. The latest information, from a grizzled prospector with a pack horse, was hardly ten minutes old. It dealt with gold on the Gila.

May the story speak apart with the reader, softly, but with no ungenerous motive? Softly, that this dreaming boy may not hear it? If, in that vanished year, you had spoken, in any company, the name of Ashtabula, that heavy word had checked all laughter and all song. There are few save those for whom grief made that name immortal who now remember that, in almost the last night of our Centennial Year, a transcontinental train went through a bridge at Ashtabula, and carried a hundred souls to death by water and fire. John Cecil's parents died together there. That is why, for more than a dozen years, the orphan's ways had been guided by trustees, to Europe and to Ann Arbor. And that was why John Cecil was now in Target. A month gone, Commencement and majority arrived together in the same dazzling week. And so, just a little weary of guidance, John Cecil, his own master, set forth upon his wander-year—which has not ended yet.

Another man—a grave and quiet man, tall, dark and broad-shouldered—shared the porch with John Cecil. His hair was really red, but it looked like black hair; he wore a black hat and rather gave the impression of a man in black, but in reality he had faded blue shirt, and faded blue overalls, pulled down over his boots; an inconspicuous man. He sat hunched over on a wooden bench and carved upon it a strange device—a fox-and-goose board, he told John Cecil, in answer to a direct question. To other direct questions he answered briefly, that he did not know, being himself a stranger in Target. So John Cecil abandoned him as unprofitable, and reverted to the information so recently imparted by the more voluble prospector. He mused on the sufferings, the resourcefulness and loyalty, and the final disaster of the old Spaniards who had hidden that treasure beset by savages; and how strangely that faded map, traced by the one survivor, had come down through two centuries. It was a good story. Many heads had gone to the making of it, and the years had lent it polish. But, of course, John Cecil did not know that.

A team of horses came through narrow West Street to the Plaza; behind them, not a wagon but a second team, their stretchers taut to a heavy chain; a third team, a fourth. John Cecil rose up to see, ran down the steps to see. Span by span, a twenty-horse team crossed the railroad track and filed into the Plaza, drawing an enormous, high-sided wagon. Trailed behind by a short stub of tongue was a second wagon, smaller indeed, but double-sized for all that. The driver rode the near wheel horse. A single line, with one end buckled to the saddle horn, passed forward through turret rings on the hames of each near horse—excepting only the swing team —and led at last to the bit of the near leader. A slender jockey stick crossed from the leader's bit to his mate's; the other horses pulled free and unguided, except for individual lines to each member of the swing team, just in front of the wheelers. A wide strap led from the saddle horn back to a ring at the top of the curving brake lever, ten feet long and as thick as a man's wrist. John Cecil watched with all his eyes. A water cask was slung by iron bands to the side of the trail wagon; there was a chuck box in the rear. The driver gave two gentle jerks on the long line, the leaders sidestepped to the right, obliqued and polkaed; the other teams followed, sidewise and forward at once, keeping 'ware and wide of the chain; curving majestically, the two wagons drew to a halt, close against the platform of Lindauer's store. The horses let the chain fall slack and stood at ease; the driver swung off and Lindauer bustled bareheaded to meet him. Little tufts of hair stood up to frame a bald patch on that frosted head. They shook hands warmly.

'Well, Hermie! Long time no see um!'

'Long time no see!' Lindauer echoed. 'Not since that Apache scrap. Why, Pres, that's been three years! But where's Scotty? Sick? Drunk, maybe? I knew something was wrong. He was due here yesterday.'

'Broke his leg.'

'Dear, dear! Kicked?'

'Wagon tongue. Climbing Staircase Hill; chain stiff as a crowbar, wheel hit a rock, tongue whipped around, snapped back—bingo! So I came down as emergency driver.'

'Tch! Tch! Bad hurt, is he?'

'Pretty bad. Big bone broke and the bruise hurts him worse than the bone. Eighteen tons of ore back of that tongue and twelve tons of horses in front—that strikes a pretty stiff blow.'

'That makes three times I've known it to happen that way,' said Lindauer soberly. 'Three times to my own knowledge. In rough country they aim to keep their feet high, or else ride sideways. But they forget. Poor Scotty! He'll have a siege of it. Of course, his pay goes on, and his expenses. Scotty knows that. . . . How about it, Pres? You want to stick till Scotty's up and around again?'

'Shucks, no. Just came down to oblige. I'm no freighter. I'm a blacksmith, me. Freighting don't appeal to me at all. Too much like work. I hope you have your man all ready to load this ore on the car. I don't hanker for it.'

'No car,' said Lindauer. 'Rotten service. Should

have been here yesterday. Drive over in the feed corral, Pres. Unhitch and feed. By that time I'll have a man to take over—Jake Blun or somebody.'

'Why not make camp and hobble 'em, if you have to wait for your car? Plenty grass, and feed costs money.'

'Plenty grass, but harness costs money,' said the merchant. 'Target has gone bad since you were here. They'd steal harness, ore, chains and wagons, unless there was someone on the job night and day! Not like old times. It's disgusting. Let me know when you're ready, and I'll send you back in the stage.'

Pres shook his head. 'Not going back—not straight off. I'm tired of blacksmithing, seems like. I got me three copper claims and a shack at Jim River, and I aim to mosey up there and do assessment work. Bimeby, after I investigate a little.'

'Jim River? Never heard of it.'

Pres Lewis twisted a silky brown beard. 'Over on the Gavilan, in the roughs. Jim River is just about as long as your freight team, and a foot wide.' He examined his hobnailed shoes and looked up sheepishly. 'You see, I was born on the James River,' he explained, 'in Virginia. Some time since.'

'I see,' said Herman. His old eyes rolled slowly from end to end of Lindauer Place—very much as if he were casting about for another name to give it.

Continuing that slow circle, the freight wagon made a complete turn and recrossed the railroad tracks. Forty sharp ears pricked up and canted alertly toward the great gates of Gray's Feed Corral, and eighty eager feet reached out briskly to that haven of lucky horses.

In the corral, Pres Lewis was just dropping the first traces, when a pleasant young voice spoke beside him.

'I beg your pardon,' said the pleasant young voice, 'but would you let me help you unharness, and then let me ask you some questions? About the freighting and the horses. I know how to manage two horses, but how about twenty? There are so many things I want to know,' said the young voice, rather breathlessly. 'How you train them, and how much you can haul, and how far you come, and what the ore is worth. I don't know anything about this country, you see; and there is so much to learn. I'll be awfully obliged if you'll tell me about things. My name is John Cecil Calvert.' He pronounced it Kolvert.

The driver's lifted eyes, large and slow and smoky-brown, saw a pleasant young face, an eager young face. He pulled a small memorandum book from a hip pocket of his blue overalls, thumbed the pages forward and back, and scanned one page closely. 'My name is—Lewis,' he said haltingly. He held the book nearer his eyes and peered again: 'Pres Lewis,' he added. 'Pres Lewis, the experienced man, who, out of the goodness of his heart, dispenses vast quantities of information gratis, like free lunch and salvation. . . . Well, unhitch a span at a time and let 'em go. We'll unharness in the stalls. Now, just what was it you wanted to know?'

'First of all, I suppose that's the reason for these big open squares, isn't it? So these long freight outfits can have room to turn around? I saw these great squares—plazas, is it?—in Santa Fé and Socorro. But I didn't happen to see any twenty-horse teams there.'

Pres Lewis stopped work and stared at his questioner. To tell the truth, the experienced man was somewhat taken aback. 'Frank John,' said he, 'I'll be honest with you. Leastways, as honest as I can be, after all these years. I've been watching freight teams turn around in these plazas ever since you was a baby, and never once thought why the plaza was made big. I thought they was just a habit. And here you've guessed how come, first off. One reason, anyway. There would be other reasons. And if you should ask me, Frank John ——'

'My name is John Cecil Calvert,' the young man spoke coldly.

Pres waved the protest aside. 'Yes, yes; I heard you. And if you can use your eyes and your brains to such good effect, you can find out nearly anything you want to know, with a little patience, without asking questions. Perhaps I ought to tell you, Frank John, that asking questions is not fashionable in these parts.'

'Why?' said Frank John.

CHAPTER IV

TWENTY HORSES were unharnessed, watered, fed with good grama hay and Kansas corn; and Frank John had learned much. Twenty names; from Prince and Charlie, the swing team, to Tom and Jerry, the leaders; with Frank John's own explanation—the correct one—as to why the mate of any Charlie horse is always Prince. How the swing team, on short curves, hopped the chain and pulled the end of the tongue at almost a right angle to the pull of the chain, and why. How the trail wagon was dropped, for deep sand and high, hard hills; how it was coupled on again; and how hard it was to do that little stunt with no swamper to help; how sad a thing it was to be a swamper. Armed with curry-comb and brush, they were smoothing over sweat-salted shoulders, and the older man was imparting other lore of the road, when a hurly-burly of shouts and laughter arose from an inner corral. At the same time, Lon Gray, owner of the feed corral, crossed behind the stalls.

Pres called to him, 'Hi, Lon; what's going on in the other pen?'

'Johnny Pardee topping off a bronc',' Gray answered indifferently.

'Frank John, you seen any horses broke yet?' said Pres. . . . 'No? Come on, then. We'll finish the currying later.'

Well-dressed onlookers sat on the gate, so the newcomers climbed over. A laughing crowd shouted encouragement to a mouse-colored horse that pitched a frantic circle, making the stirrups pop with every pitch. Most of them knew Pres Lewis and roared greetings to him—Erie Patterson with three of his men, Dave Salt, Newt Somers and Bartolome Pino; Tolson the assayer; Nash, the grocer; Hugh Monro, of the bridge gang; Breen, McKee and Goddard, miners from Argentine; Jim Yewell, the town marshal, and Steve Davis, the sheriff. There were some whom Lewis did not know—two who seemed to be 'drummers,' and a well-dressed, round man with a plump, pink face and a gray goatee. These three sat on the gate, and Pres noted a fourth stranger inside, a broad-shouldered man who leaned against the gatepost and whittled on a yucca stalk, with his head bent to watch his handiwork, so that a black hat brim flopped over his eyes; a man in two shades of faded blue, a man with red hair that pretended to be black.

'Oh, lookit Johnny Pardee, with new chaps and shiny conchos on 'em!' said Pres. 'Ain't he just too sweet? All he lacks is a snakeskin hatband and a coupla guns. Nice nag you got there, Johnny. Your horse?'

'Naw, I'm just breaking him. He belongs to Mr. Hawkins, there.' He jerked his chin at the whittler.

That person raised his head and glanced out from under his flopping hat brim.

'That statement isn't exactly right,' he corrected mildly. 'The little *grullo* still belongs to Mr. Patterson. If he gentles down and quits bucking for keeps, I buy him. But if his heart is real bad, he's no mount for old Bill Hawkins, and Mr. Patterson keeps him and sells me a kind one. . . . That right, Mr. Patterson?'

'That's the deal,' said Patterson. 'Personally, I hope the *grullo* don't gentle to suit you. I like his looks, and I priced him too cheap to you.'

The mouse-colored horse desisted from his exercises, snorted loudly, ran on the rope experimentally, whirled at the rope's end, and faced his captor, head up, but slightly a tremble. Johnny walked toward him slowly, patiently, coiling the rope as he went. With low and soothing speech he put out his hand toward a black nose; after two slight flurries, was able to pat that nose, to rub the dark head gently. 'His name is Smoky, I think,' said Johnny softly, and without turning his head. His left hand, holding the coiled rope, slipped up and closed firmly around the cheek piece of the bridle, his right hand moved slowly to the saddle horn, his foot was in the stirrup. Johnny eased into the saddle smoothly, loosened his hold on the cheek piece, held the hackamore reins taut, and patted the quivering neck. 'Come, boy! C-chk!' Smoky made two cautious sidewise steps, three ——

'Whoopee!' Dave Salt shouted, and sent his big gray sombrero sailing through the air into the bronco's face. The bronco fairly screamed with fright as he went up into the air, and fence-railed, bawling, across the corral, zigzag bucking. Johnny rode easily, surely, as if he were part of the horse. Three jumps, four, five —— At the next plunge, saddle and man left the horse's back together; the hind cinch held for a second, the horse twisted and plunged, saddle and Johnny rolled in the dust together.

Smoky leaped high in air, twisted zigzag again and came down almost on top of his fallen rider. He bucked again, stiff-legged, bawling, straight up and straight down; he bunched all his feet together

Whoopee!

Courtesy Ruth Koerner Oliver

and lit fairly on Johnny's thigh. His feet slipped from the thick leggins. Men ran toward him, shouting. The horse was high in air again, head between his feet. Johnny tried to crawl and roll from under. Again those bunched feet slid from the protecting leggins. The horse dropped and lay still. Johnny rolled clear, half dragged by grasping hands.

'You hurt, Johnny?' gasped Munro, who was the nearest.

'Don't think so. Scared. Them leggins saved my bacon, that time.'

'Who fired that shot?' Those thunder tones were the town marshal's. Frank John remembered then, vaguely, that he had heard a shot somewhere. Oh! Was that why the mouse-colored horse lay so still? 'Who fired that gun, I say? I've warned you fellows not to pack your guns in town.'

'Oh, to hell with your guns, and you too!' said Hugh Munro. He glared upon authority with a hard eye. Here the plump old gentleman climbed down on the other side of the gate and departed. The 'drummers' followed him. 'Here's a boy barely missed a most unpleasant death, and you can't wait to see if his leg's broke or what, before you go to blowing off your empty head about guns. Tough on that poor devil of a horse—but suppose he'd come down on Johnny's belly?'

'I tell you this gun-toting has got to stop. The law ——'

'Shut up, you windbag! . . . How about it, Johnny? Leg broke?'

'Guess not. Help me up.' Johnny stood up and experimented shakily. 'Nothing broke. Just scared. Not so bad bruised, either. Them good old chaps, they're next thing to armor.' He hobbled painfully to his saddle.

Pres Lewis spoke up then, in a mild and honeyed voice, 'That gun, now, Mr. Marshal—that was me. I couldn't see Johnny killed, trifling as he is. Humph! Jim Yewell, marshal, "with a star on his breast and a sir to his name." I wasn't knowin' to your new dignities, fair sir and Mr. Marshal—not till after I done shot and some kind friend showed me your star. You was just lookout for a faro game when I knew you.'

'But you can't carry guns in this town,' said the sheriff heavily. 'That's final. We're going to enforce the law.'

'Now, now, sheriff; go easy. I've just nicely got in. Not five minutes since I unharnessed. I know your new law. I've got a right to carry a gun on the road for protection, and I haven't been in a house yet. Just got unharnessed.'

'You give me that gun!' thundered Marshal Yewell.

Lewis took a square of plug tobacco from his pocket, scrutinized it, selected a corner and gnawed a segment from it. 'You keep your voice down, brother,' he said, restoring the mutilated plug to its pocket. 'If you bellow at me any more I'm liable to prophesy against you. You just turn your mind back and see what happened when people crowded me into foretelling. When you got any communications for me, I want 'em sweet and low, like the wind of the western sea. You remember that. And that gun—well, whilst you and Mr. Munro was conversing together, I passed that gun through the gate to old Lon and told him to keep it for me in the office. So that's all right. I don't want to hear any more about that gun.'

Frank John's eyes were bulging. His new and kindly friend was an unblushing liar. Lewis was in his short sleeves, he had worn no gun; starting quicker, he had been in front of Frank John as the shot was fired, when both were plunging in to help the luckless Pardee. Moreover, that man Lon Gray had been at the gate in time to hear the second lie, which concerned him; hearing it, he had nodded his gray head and turned back to the office. Partners in iniquity! Doubtless this man Gray would have a pistol ready to match the lie, with an empty shell to represent the one which had ended life for the luckless horse.... But, after all, who had fired that shot?

'All right, Lewis,' said Erie Patterson smoothly. 'Nobody's going to make any trouble about that gun, of course. It's a good thing for young Pardee you hadn't put it up yet.'

'Only, if you can shoot like that,' said the sheriff, 'you may look to be called on a posse, 'most any time. That horse was hit plumb between the eyes. I got a wire last night that Bill Doolin was seen this side of Roswell, coming this way. He's wanted, five thousand dollars' worth. So maybe I'll have use for you and your gun.'

'Bill Doolin?' echoed Lewis blankly.

'Why, man; surely you've heard of Bill Doolin—train robber, bank robber? The Indian Territory was always the wild spot on any map. Forty-eight deputy United States marshals killed there in four years. One marshal a month. Tough men in the territory, and Doolin is the toughest and the shrewdest. But here lately they've been making the Nations too hot to hold him.'

'I been in the high country, blacksmithing and mining,' said Lewis apologetically. 'I never heard about the Centennial till day before yesterday.'

'There is one point which has not yet been touched upon,' said Patterson. 'Just who pays for my horse?' He glanced at Pres Lewis as he spoke.

'I'm sorry for your loss, Mr. Patterson, and I'm a good deal sorrier for that *grullo* horse. His splendid days are over. And it wasn't his fault at all. He was trying to understand, that bronc' was; hoping it would turn out all right. Then somebody sailed a hat at him. I'd like to pay for that horse; I would so. But I promised not to do that. Never. Promised faithfully. Why not let him pay that made the trouble? . . . Who's bareheaded?'

Dave Salt was bareheaded—Erie Patterson's straw boss, reputed to be a tough citizen. He looked the part. 'I didn't mean any harm,' he said. 'Just wanted to see a little fun. Where is my hat, anyway?'

It was Hawkins, the big man with the black hat, who answered this question. He sat quietly on the dead horse, still whittling. He pointed with his knife to a spot midway between himself and Johnny Pardee, who sat upon his saddle blankets, feeling cautiously on his injured leg.

Dave Salt broke into a wild roaring, half howl and half bellow. 'My new hat! Cut in four pieces! I'll have blood for this!'

The big man looked up with smiling, kindly eyes.

Hawkins

Courtesy Ruth Koerner Oliver

'I hope you don't suspect me, just because I was setting here handy with my knife open.'

Johnny Pardee rose and limped painfully to his saddle. 'Look at this, Salt! You're not the only one hurt. Someone has been mighty free with a knife before ever you threw your hat. See this off latigo of mine? Someone cut it where it doubles over the ring—cut it almost through, so it was bound to bust in three or four jumps. See it?'

'You little runt; you did this?' snarled Salt. He leaned in act to step.

But the man Hawkins moved noiselessly and spoke now into Dave Salt's ear. 'On the other hand, neighbor,' he said softly, 'your hat seems to have been worked on by a very sharp knife. Now, my knife is very sharp. See it?' He held the knife out for inspection. For that purpose he reached over Dave's shoulder, holding the knife about one inch from Dave's jugular vein. Simultaneously, his left hand reached under Dave's coat and abstracted a .45-caliber revolver from a holster stuck under the waistband of Dave's natty doeskins; he tossed it back to a snappy double play—Breen to McKee to Munro. Munro shoved it under his coat. 'Under the circumstances,' sighed Bill Hawkins regretfully, 'sooner than have you jump on to a cripple half your size, perhaps I had better take the blame for your hat. Any objections?'

'I cut up the hat meself,' snapped Breen. 'Out of respect for the horse—poor baste! By way of mourning, like!'

'Here!' cried a loud voice by the gate. 'I want this squabbling stopped, right now. Hear me!' Slim Jack Farr sat his horse without, and looked over the gate. 'Sheriff there? And the marshal? You're both wanted, right off.'

'What is it? A shooting scrape?' said the sheriff, making for the gate.

'Next thing to it. There's an old geezer over to the stockyards with a bunch of cattle to water. And he's trying to force the station agent, Mr. Wade Barton—you know him, Erie—he's trying to make the agent take pay for that water—five cents a head. Barton refused to take any money, and he's afraid Carmody—that's this old codger with the cows—is going to use violence to force this money on him. You'd better come over and protect him.'

Peaceful assayer, peaceful grocer, had oozed unnoticed, long since. The lawlike faction, officers and the four Ladder men, departed together, crestfallen, defied, muttering and malcontent. The miners went next, loftily, nose in air, followed by the painful progress of young Pardee, aided by

Breen's shoulder on the left and Munro's on the right; the latter openly carrying Dave Salt's gun as spoil of war. Pres Lewis and his pupil were left alone.

Pres looked down at the dead horse. He bent to stroke the dark head, once only, but not ungently. 'Poor fellow!' said Pres. 'That was hard luck! All over now! Come on, Frank John, you'll be wanting to go to the water pen for a squint at that herd and the chuck wagon, and so on. I'll finish up the currying.'

Young Frank John gave his head a shaking then, and stretched himself. 'I feel like one who treads alone, Mr. Lewis, some banquet hall deserted,' said Frank John. 'Before I go, you might tell me, as between one gentleman and a blacksmith—who shot that horse?'

CHAPTER V

'WHAT was all that goose grease Elmer was giving us?' asked Pres. He sat at supper with Johnny Pardee in the big dining room of the Holland House. The room was crowded with hungry and noisy people; these two were at a small table near a window.

'What was who giving us?'

'Old Elmer—Elmer Farr.'

'Jack Farr? You're always calling people out of their names. Disrespectful. That Michigan kid spoke real bitter about it.'

'Who—Frank John? You been getting acquainted with Frank John?'

'He has my family history ever since Columbus crossed the Delaware,' said Johnny. 'When I quit him, he was getting statistics about the B 4 outfit. Persistent cuss!'

'So am I,' said Pres. 'Information is what I'm after. Passing lightly over the point that old Elmer's name is really Elmer Farr and not Jack Farr.'

'I declare, I'd forgotten that,' said Johnny. 'Jack, we call him, and Slim. Say, Mr. Lewis, who do you suppose cut my cinch? That was sure one dirty trick, if ever I knew one. I think it was Dave Salt himself. One of the Ladder men, anyhow. They was all there while I was getting a hackamore on that unlucky horse and teaching him to lead a little. Them Ladders is due for a showdown. They've been crowding all us little fellows nine ways from the jack. I've had an elegant sufficiency myself.'

'Be that as it may, beloved, will you, Johnny Pardee, now tell me, Pres Lewis, just exactly what Slim Jack Elmer Farr meant by that windy about somebody paying for water for them dogies? Take your time, me laddie buck. Only bear in mind what I just said. Perhaps I would do better to explain that the reason that I ask you is because I want to know.'

'In that case,' said Johnny, 'I'll tell you; although you may possibly have noticed that us cowmen don't consult much with miners and railroaders and storekeepers and freighters and sheep herders and blacksmiths—that sort of people. Of course, we think they ought to be allowed to vote, and pay taxes, and so on; or maybe we buy 'em a drink when we feel good-natured and mellow, but we don't really consider them overmuch in our calculations.'

'You give me no news. Many's the laugh we have at your airs and graces. But if some people—people with a fairly good opinion of themselves, too—if they knew half what I know about them——'

Johnny held up his hand. 'Oh, in that case, I'll tell you. It was like this.' His voice sank to an undertone. It was a long telling.

'Uh-huh! So you and Elmer think the Ladder outfit aim to bedevil——'

'Jack Farr thinks, and I just back his play to the limit. If this Carmody man gives any excuse for these buzzards to sic the law on him, he's right in the middle of a bad fix. His cattle can just nicely keep their feet; and they've got to lay over a spell, come hell or high water. Me and Farr and our bunch, we aim to help Carmody herd 'em—to make sure he doesn't have trouble shoved on him—while we're studying how about it, and what next. He ain't got no money, either. This Bill Hawkins, that I was breaking the pony for, he bought one of Carmody's top horses this evening. I reckon that's every cent the old chap has to his name.'

'How come his horses ain't poor, too?' said Lewis.

'Shucks! Carmody himself, he's right chunky. But the crew is just three kids out of the cradle, and Charlie Bird, the right bower. He's a little dried-up old herring, no bigger'n a pint of cider. That cavvyard is in right good shape. Thin, but peart.'

'Well,' said Pres judicially, 'if you will insist on bringing your troubles to me, I suppose I'll have to take charge.' Here Johnny sniffed. Pres regarded him austerely for a moment, and then continued: 'Why don't you take this herd out to your ranch? Or why don't some of your crowd do it—whichever one has the best lay?'

'That's what it comes to—there or thereabouts. Those cattle are in no shape to tackle what's waitin' for 'em west of Heartbreak Hill. And let me tell you, mister, right then is where and when sorrow begins. The Gridiron has been all crosswise this long time—the Ladders and the Rockingchair on one side, and us little fellows on the other. The Chair outfit isn't so bad, but Patterson has been siding in with Troy Ware on every little friction and dispute, and muched him along till Troy thinks Erie is just as fine as silk. And Troy's riders are hard hombres. Trouble brewing. This Carmody play will just about bring it to a boil. They claim we run more cattle already than we got water for. And we don't stack up very well. Ladders and Chairs, they make just even twenty; lacking some three, or maybe four, that'll quit 'em when they begin dealin' from the bottom. And a lot of money. And the sheriff. And the town marshal. And the tinhorn vote, maybe. Aid and comfort and God knows what else, from some of the railroaders. Us fellows—let me see; Farr, Dal Cline, Aurelio Sais and me—that's four—and Cat Knapp and that Englishman, Carbray, and Larry Denny, that works for Carbray—seven of us, all told. The Packsaddle men are all on a big pasear down in Mexico and won't be back till round-up time.'

'Vent slips!' said Lewis. 'And the three punchers that you expect to quit when the dirty work starts—three good men—that's eleven, and this upstanding Munro and me, that makes sixteen. What can be fairer than that? Not to mention Carmody himself, and his little old hired man.'

'That listens fine,' said Johnny. 'But you know what happened to the ten little niggers standing in a line?'

'Something happened—I don't just recollect what,' said Lewis, frowning with the effort to remember. 'And then there were but nine.'

Johnny nodded. 'And so on. That's the idea. We don't want to start anything. They'll start it. At night, or from a dry gulch. And then we'll lose on the first clash. Our best men, likely.'

'Oh, I'll be cautious,' said Pres.

Johnny ignored this levity and proceeded with a gloomy face: 'I don't like it, just because I've naturally got good sense. What is more to the point, Jack Farr don't like it, either; nor Aurelio Sais—and both of 'em have been through one or two of these things already. Oh, why can't people have some sense?'

'I have,' said Pres grandly. 'It shall never be said that you sought help and leadership from me in vain. You know Jim River?'

'Jim River? Aw, what kind of guff are you springing now?'

'No guff. This is good medicine. Jim River's mine. Over in the Gavilan, beyond Farr's layout. Mighty few have been there. Jim River is maybe fifty yards long, an inch deep, and one mouse jump across. Rough, but good grass, good browse, plenty water, plenty mountain lions and bear. Them dogies will do fine there, if the old man will rustle himself two or three hound dogs and chase the varmints out.'

'Out onto us?' suggested Johnny.

Pres considered this. 'There may be something to that,' he admitted. 'All right. Then you get some hounds and chase 'em elsewhere. Kill 'em when you tree 'em. Good practice for the great day a-coming. The big point is, this wise and wary scheme will postpone that great day till you're better fixed. Jim

River is over the divide. Not one of these cattle need ever range in Gridiron, and so your two cattle companies won't have any grievance.'

'Terms?' said Johnny.

'Let's see. This is August. Here's the lay: The B 4 brand can run at Jim River until after steer selling, next spring, for no dollars and no cents. After that, if the old man wants to stick around, we can dicker. If he elects to go on, it won't cost him nary a cent. To be sure, if he sees fit to build a wagon road, I'll never tear it down. In the meantime, he'll have to pack in his provender. Oh, yes. Deer and quail and rabbits. Right good shack too. Two-room rock house. Dirt roof.'

'This is right clever of you, Mr. Lewis.'

'Isn't it?' said Mr. Lewis enthusiastically. 'Isn't that just like me? You don't half know how fine it is, either. I was planning on something quite different. I've always tried to lead an honest life, and now I'm little better than a cowman. But maybe Carmody'll move on. It's pretty rough in there, and lonesome. I sorter intended to do a little counterfeiting there this winter. Oh, well! At any rate, this will give your crowd time to practice shooting, against the hour of need.'

'I knew I was forgetting something,' said Johnny, pushing back his plate. 'Who was it shot that horse?'

'I didn't see. But when questions was asked and nobody spoke up, I judged that whoever it was had his reasons. Nobody had anything on me, so I up and claims the glory.'

'Oh, I knew it wasn't you. I saw your work with a six-shooter once. Didn't know that, did you? I was about ten or twelve years old and quiet for my age. Over at Ojo Caliente, before they moved the Apaches from there and started all this hell we been having. . . . Now, this horse, he was shot smack through the brain pan, and him bucking. That let you out, and every other man I ever knew, barring two or three.'

'I see!' said Pres Lewis. 'You think it was the pink, fat man on the gate? With the goatee and the linen duster?' His eyes roved the dining hall as he spoke, and rested for a little on Mr. Hawkins, who sat alone in the rear at a corner table, with his back to the wall. Johnny's glance followed his; Mr. Hawkins was eating busily, but he looked up at this juncture. Pres waved a slight salute, which Hawkins acknowledged with a nod. Pres turned to face Johnny then. Their eyes met.

'This horse that 'Enry 'Awkins bought—was he a good one?'

'His name is Bill, not Henry,' corrected Johnny. 'That horse? A tough one, anyway. And gentle. He got one of these smoke-colored horses, and I never saw one yet but was a stayer.'

'Gunwise?'

'Benefactor, chieftain, Great White Father, I didn't hear the trade made. But I'll make a little wager with you. I'll bet you twenty good dollars, current with the merchant, to one of your own make, that the new Hawkins horse is gunwise.'

'Trust 'Enry for that! No, Mr. Pardee, I couldn't make that bet. Thank you just the same. And I need the money too. . . . 'Enry looks to me like a good man,' said Pres. 'Yes, sir, if I needed a good man right bad, I'd take a chance on 'Enry. By the way, who was that quartered out Salt friend's hat?'

'I didn't see,' said Johnny.

'I don't feel hungry at all,' said Pres. 'Can you make out to ride a right gentle horse without hurting your leg too much? 'Cause if you can, let's you and me ride over to the bed ground and carry the good news. Spring Jim River on your friend—or was it your friend's friend? And hadn't you or Farr or somebody better tell Patterson that if the herd can lay over three days, real peaceful and quiet, Carmody will move them on, then? It may save trouble. If Carmody tells 'em, they'll frame up a fight on him, sure.'

'Farr is hitting up the booze. I wish he wouldn't,' said Johnny. 'He's ugly. Dangerous to enemies, friends, strangers and himself. Leave him be. And they don't like me much. I'll get Aurelio to tell 'em tomorrow. They're superstitious about Aurelio. If he advises 'em to lay off, they'll consider it. But why three days? Wouldn't it be shrewd and knowing to get that herd away right sudden and soon? . . . Ps-st! Hold everything! Here comes the sheriff.'

Steve Davis came ponderously between the tables, with Patterson and Troy Ware in his wake. Ware was general manager of the Rockingchair outfit, the biggest cattle company in those parts. North Gridiron was half of the Rockingchair range. The other half lay north beyond the mountains, on the Feliz and the Gato.

The two cattlemen were smiling, but the sheriff's heavy face was worried. He was holding a yellow telegram in his hand.

'Gentlemen, I may need you on my posse sure enough. I wish you wouldn't leave town. I just had another wire. Bill Doolin was seen near Palomas Hot Springs, yesterday was a week ago. Positively identified.'

'Doolin is bothered with rheumatism, it seems,' said Troy Ware, 'and it is thought that he would have stayed near the springs if unmolested. But they went there to look for him—and now where is he?'

'Read this wire, Mr. Lewis,' said the sheriff. 'Now, it's like this: I'm keeping good men on the lookout in every settlement, and if he comes into my bailiwick, we're going to stop everything and get him.'

'I'm crippled,' said Johnny. 'Leave me out.'

'I have married me a yoke of oxen and a vineyard——' Pres began.

'That's enough, Mr. Lewis. You will consider yourself a member of my posse. I need men like you. Your pay starts in the morning. Stay here in town until further developments. . . . As for you, Johnny, I'll have to send the doctor to look at that leg.'

'Doctor, my foot! You come to my room and see for yourself. I'm black and blue from my knee to my hip, and you make it worse. You saw that horse jump on me. I'm going home in a buckboard, that's where I'm going.'

'Steve, I guess there's no doubt but what the boy is hurt,' said Erie Patterson, smiling. 'There's plenty without him.'

'All right, then. But you're done made a deputy, Mr. Lewis. Hold yourself in readiness for duty.' Following the cattlemen, he made for the saloon door.

Steve Davis, Sheriff

Courtesy Ruth Koerner Oliver

' "So shines a good deed in a naughty world," ' said Pres. 'See what I get for being a crack shot. Come on, Johnny; I got a horse tied out there for you. Say, this will be a joke on the sheriff if he sticks me up to shoot it out with Bill Doolin on the strength of one accidental shot.'

'It'll be a joke on somebody,' said Johnny, as they went out into the falling dusk.

'About that unanswered question,' said Pres, as they rode along slowly down the deserted street. ' "Why three days?" says you. Because I think your friend Carmody ought to ride out to take a look at Jim River before he takes his cattle in there. When I say it's rough, what I mean is that it's sure-enough rough. Say, you've been through Soledad Canyon, east of Las Cruces? I know you have; heard you tell about visiting Jeff Isaacks there. Well, Jim River is like that, and more so. Why, Johnny, right behind my house there's a pinky granite needle half a mile up—straight up—one side sharp like another, slick as glass. That thing must have shoved up all at once, right through the crust, like you'd stick a knife through a tambourine. That was long ago,' said Pres. 'There were no gods then, and circles had no centers.'

CHAPTER VI

IT WAS PAST EIGHT when the news bearers returned. Their business had been of the briefest. 'Jim River listens good,' said Carmody. 'I owe you a day in harvest. Maybe you'll never collect it yourself, but the worst that can happen will be that I'll do a turn for somebody else. Thankee.' Upon which, Lewis had declared for that delayed investigation.

That broad balcony of Lindauer Place was lighted by hanging lamps, square in glass and ironwork; and there a goodly portion of Target took their ease. The two friends went into the hotel lobby, finding there Troy Ware, Max Hollocher, who was the bank cashier, and Chris Holl, chatting together from the comfort of the deepest armchairs. Through the open door from the saloon floated strange sounds, as of one who bellowed a lullaby:

Oh, the Prodigal Son was a son of a gun!
He was! He was!
He shuffled the cards and he played for mon!
He did! He did!

'Hark!' said Johnny. 'Don't I hear something? Is it—can it be——'

'It is,' said Chris Holl. 'Jack Farr, just as drunk as he can be. Of course, when I say "drunk," I don't mean really drunk. I never saw Elmer unconscious.'

'I could do with a drink myself,' said Pres. 'But I don't want to get tangled up with no drunks. Let's slip through into the back and make signs to the bar creature. Won't you boys join us?'

The boys excused themselves with thanks. Farr was noisy at the bar, with townsmen and several of the Ladders assisting. Their passing was unnoticed. In the rear they noted, together with hilarious tables of pitch, seven-up, solo, and a quiet, four-handed poker game. The players were Blondy Black, Eastman Hall and Sam Clark—three youths who would in time be tinhorn gamblers—and for the fourth none other than young Frank John, who was enjoying himself very much. They were all boys. Young Sam Clark—Lithpin Tham—was even younger than Frank John. The newcomers took a near-by table, and, for a starter, investigated the beer. The big poker games were in private rooms at the back, where, through the open transom, Erie Patterson and the sheriff were audible.

For Johnny and Pres, investigation of spiced rum followed, with a preliminary round of seven-up to see who should pay for it. After which the investigators passed into Lindauer's store, where business was brisk.

'They're trimming the lad,' said Johnny. 'They're letting him win on purpose now. Blondy called him once and our visiting friend showed down kings and fours. Blondy threw in his hand and Frank John raked the pot. But I saw Blondy's cards, and he had aces up.'

'Sure, I saw that,' said Pres. 'We'll horn in. Listen!' Johnny listened; and thereafter Pres sought out Lindauer and, when his turn came, spoke aside with him:

'Hermie, I'm out of money. Can I borrow some of your shiny new bank?'

'Certainly, my friend. First thing in the morning.'

'No, no,' said Pres. 'I want it tonight. About two hundred, maybe. Till my ship comes in.'

'Against the rules, Pres. Office hours, nine to four. We got to keep our own rules, ain't it? Same with the notes. If you own real estate—not squatter's right, but patented land, or town lots—then we lend on your name. But if you own no land yourself, you must have a landowner's indorsement.'

'That's a hell of a note,' said Pres, embarrassed. 'I don't own no land, and well you know it. Why,

Hermie, it's your bank, isn't it? You're the president. You know I'll pay you back, don't you?'

'Sure, sure,' said the banker. 'But we are not lending our own money. It is the stockholders' money, the depositors' money, and we must hold to the safeguards agreed upon. All this is well understood in older countries, but here you are like children yet.'

'Oh, well, lend it to me yourself.'

'But I can't do that,' said Lindauer. 'The stockholders and officers are bound not to lend money themselves, or to go on any man's note.'

'Why, Hermie!' The would-be borrower's face was both crestfallen and pained.

'Now, Pres! Now, Pres!' protested Hermie. 'Don't you see, it's got to be that way? Just as we may not borrow for ourselves from our own bank. No, you get Cline, or Sais, or some other friend to go on your note, and that will be O.K.'

'Oh, well. . . . I suppose I can get a bill of goods on tick, anyway?'

'Anything in the store, old friend,' said Lindauer, much relieved. 'You must not take it amiss—what I said. It is the custom. You are not used to banking yet, ain't it?'

Lewis took out a stub of a pencil, rolled his eyes

for better consideration, and presently handed his old friend a brief list:

> 2 packs star-backed playing cards
> 20 five-dollar bills
> 10 ten-dollar bills
> Charge to acct. of
> P. B. LEWIS

Lindauer viewed these items with starting eyes. 'All ridght! All ridght!' he cried, and threw up both hands. 'Robber, I'll fill your bill myself! Come back to the safe. Such a man!'

Pres divided his purchases fairly with Pardee. After a whispered consultation they trooped back into the Gem and halted beside the poker table.

'Any room for two good players? Who's the banker? What's the come-in?' demanded Johnny.

'Free for all. Ten dollars come-in. All jackpots,' said Eastman Hall civilly, but without enthusiasm.

The newcomers drew up chairs between Frank John and Lithpin Tham. With a flourish, Johnny spread out a neat bunch of greenbacks. 'I'm playing this much behind my stack,' he announced.

'Same here,' said Lewis.

'You know, this is just a friendly little game,' remonstrated Blondy. 'You don't want to go to bulling it.'

'Oh, no, nothing like that,' said Pres. 'Just want

to be able to tap the winners, so long as I can. I expect to do my playing mostly with Pardee, anyhow. Got it in for him.'

It was even so. The newcomers made no splurge, played a few pots, made no raises, and stayed about even with the board; not without pointed comment. Several rounds passed with the mill run of hands. Then, Pres Lewis dealing, Frank John and his original playmates passed in turn. Johnny opened for three dollars. Pres raised him seven. Frank John, Blondy, Hall and Lithpin Tham passed in turn. Johnny shoved in seven dollars, considered, and raised back for ten.

'I'll see that,' said Pres. 'Cards, if any?'

'Three right off the top,' said Johnny.

'And three to me,' said Pres. 'Your bet, my son.'

'Ten,' said Johnny.

'And ten more.'

'And ten better,' said Johnny.

'Call you.' Pres pushed his money in without hesitation. 'That's all I got in front of me, barrin' a few white chips. What you got?'

'Queens.'

The older man's face fell perceptibly. 'How many?' he questioned gloomily.

'Two.'

'That's good,' said Pres heavily.

Johnny showed them to him—two queens and three trash cards. Lewis tossed in his hand. 'Gimme another stack, banker,' said he, and laid another roll of bills on the table.

Four stunned gamblers gazed on one another with a wild surmise. 'That is magnificent,' murmured Frank John, 'but it is not poker.'

Blondy Black leaned over the table. 'The house rules—we forgot to tell you—the house rules are that the left bower beats big casino and you can't trump your partner's ace with pinochle unless high and low will put you out.'

Lewis plucked up spirit. 'That's all right; I'm just baiting Johnny along. I'll get him presently and go south with him.'

Cautious playing followed. The first comers were distrustful, having no desire to get tangled in another orgy of wild betting. Only a few hands elapsed until, with Lewis dealing, the pot was passed up to Pardee again. He opened, and Pres Lewis raised him ten. The four other men passed out. Johnny started to throw his hand in the deck, reconsidered, studied, picked up a ten-dollar bill, all but dropped it in the pot, drew it back, folded it, creased it, refolded it to a lamplighter, and finally took up another bill of the same dimensions and pushed both in the pot.

'See that and raise you ten,' said Pres.

'Ten right back at you.'

' "Another for Hector," ' said Pres. 'Your ten and my ten, which is all the tens in stock at the present writing. Only this time I shove in my few but useful white checks.'

'I call that,' said Johnny.

Pres picked up the cards. 'How many?'

'Help yourself.'

Pres laid the pack down. 'All right. What have you got?'

'Not at all. What have you got? I called you.'

'Oh, just a flush.'

'Same here,' said Johnny. 'Only this is a straight flush.'

'Mine is a straight flush too,' Lewis confessed. 'How high is yours?'

'Just a little one. Ace high.'

'Mine is ace high too,' said Pres, absently. He raised guileless eyes to meet Johnny's. 'I suppose you know that, in case of ties, spades outrank the other suits. It doesn't often happen, but them's the rules. Spades, hearts, diamonds, clubs.'

'I never heard of such a rule in my life,' said Johnny, 'and I doubt if anybody else ever did. But that suits me. Here's mine.' He laid down the ace, king, queen, jack and ten of spades.

'That's odd,' said Pres. To the shocked gaze of the noncombatants he spread out a black fan of spades—ace, king, queen, jack and ten.

'Well, well! It's a tie!' said Johnny without emotion. 'We'll have to divide the pot.' Lewis shoved his hand into the discard and Johnny's five cards went in with them; they fell to dividing the pot.

'Fellows, I got to go,' said Eastman Hall in a cracked and horrified voice. 'Cash in. I am not feeling well at all.'

'Thith ith thure going to be a lethon to me,' said Lithpin Tham.

'But I don't understand,' said Frank John, bewildered. Lewis and Pardee had departed to return, as unsatisfactory, the money advanced by Lindauer. Lithpin Tham and Hall were seeking forgetfulness at the bar. 'They weren't trying to get our money. To all intents and purposes, they only played those two hands with each other. What was the idea?'

'Well, I'll tell you,' said Blondy Black. 'We was leading you on, see? Baiting you. We wasn't cheating you, because there was no necessity of it. Suppose when you started in tonight you lost your first ten-dollar stack, and then another stack, and then another—why, you might have got discouraged and quit, like as not. But you lost ten dollars and bought another stack and won, and had twenty dollars in front of you, and lost that, and bought another stack, and won back to thirty dollars, and so on, till you had bought forty or fifty dollars' worth, and had it about all in front of you. That was to make you think it was no difference how much you lost, because you could always win it back. Your mistake. When you get to hurrying the game and grabbing at the cards and trying to play in every pot—then you're stuck! And it don't make any difference then how much you lose, you keep on buying. That is why I am seriously considering being a professional tinhorn. It seems silly to work.'

'But what has all that got to do with this clowning? Two ace-high spade flushes—what did they gain by that?'

'Dear—oh, dear!' said Blondy. 'That was to break up the game in a nice pleasant way, without hurting anybody's feelings—so you wouldn't lose your shirt. Hey! Listen up in front! That Mr. Farr, he is making tall talk. We'd better get out of here, you and me both. This is no place for innocent young boys!'

CHAPTER VII

'TARGET ish no good town,' said Jack Farr. He stood sidewise to the bar, leaning heavily on his left elbow, so that he faced Newt Somers, Bart Pino and Dave Salt, a little farther up the bar. Farr was in his shirt sleeves, as indeed were the others, and it was evident that none of them carried guns. It was also evident, in connection with Farr's truculent face, that his befuddled mind had spotted his more calcitrant body in the position he would have chosen had he worn a gun on his right hip, with a reasonable expectancy that he might want to use it. In the long and slender fingers of his right hand, not too steadily, he held a half-filled whisky glass. 'Target ish no good town,' he repeated. 'A large housh ish unaccount'bly mishing, a shide track and a puffeckly good train of cars dishappeared overnight; a gentleman puts a mess of bread in the oven to bake, shlips away to get a small drink, and when he comesh back his stove is gone. Yesh!'

The words were painfully spaced and slow. He drank his liquor and sent the glass sliding along the bar. Then he glanced around. Ellis Kames, the lawyer, came through from the hotel, looked at Farr, sized up the situation, shrugged his shoulders and passed on through the front door without stopping for a good-night drink. Hawkins slouched inattentive in a chair against the wall. Beyond him, near the door, Marshal Yewell sat at a small table littered with newspapers. Farr turned his eyes upon the marshal and took up his tirade again:

'We got a sheriff and a tall marshal and a comfort'ble jail. What happensh? Ish that jail full of crooks? No-o-o! Somebody runsh hish horse down the street, or shings about "lonely now sheems everything"——Here, I'll shing it!' His eyes grew round; his voice was tearful and husky:

Shoon beyond the harbor bar
Shall my bark be shailing far——

The song was interrupted. The sheriff and Patterson came from the poker room, passed beyond the singer to the bar and ordered drinks. Farr glowered at the interruption. Lewis and Pardee came in from the store, the latter painfully dragging a stiffened leg. They leaned against the wall beside the door leading from the store. Frank John joined them at this observation post.

Farr lifted up his voice to address the universe in

general. 'I wash telling you,' he said. 'Sho they puts 'em in jail for shinging On the Banksh of the Old Tennesshee, or for toting gunsh. Man orter tote a gun——'

'We sometimes put drunks in jail, too,' said the marshal. As he spoke, the Gem's Jim came from the poker room where he had been banking; Jim, the proprietor, tallow-faced, wearing the black coat and white vest of the professional gambler. He stood at the end of the bar and eyed the tipsy Farr reflectively, lifting a questioning eyebrow at the marshal. The slouching Hawkins sat up straighter in his chair.

Farr fixed his disconcerting eyes upon the marshal's face. It was not a threatening glance; merely observant and thoughtful, as of one who charges his memory with something for future reference.

'Drunksh, yesh, but no thieves or housh burners. Never the one that picked the drunk mansh pocket when he's down with hish head under him.'

'I see where you are going to sleep tonight,' said the marshal.

'Can you shee no further?' jeered Farr. 'You've got a star on your vest and a gun on your hip, and I ain't got neither one. But, man, have you no mishgivingsh? Closh your eyes now, and try if you cannot shee where you and me might meet yet in a loneshome plashe, and a chill wind blowing?'

'Do you threaten me?'

'No, no! Daydreamin', thash all. Me threaten? Me? Tell you what; boy could stick live coal in corncob and run me clear out of town. And me besh man in town too. Heap the besh! For,' said Jack Farr simply, and lapsing by degrees into a barbaric chant, ' "I am a jolly baker and I bake bread brown!" No, shir, Misher Marshal, shir; you're dead right 'bout drunksh. Damn nuishance. Shoutin' an' shingin' . . .

Sho early in the morning came a knocking at my door.
Tirra, la, tirra la, lay!

"Sthurbin' peace. Thash bad! Gotter stop! But your Steve Sheriff's all wrong about gunsh. Man orter pack gun! Man gotter pack gun! Needsh gunsh where they burn down houshs and cut cinches.' He flicked a pale eye toward the three Ladder men.

'Anyone that says I cut that cinch is a damned liar!' howled Salt.

Smack! Farr's open hand slapped full on the thrusting face, punctuation to the word; pivot and arm and wrist adding speed to the blow. Salt went spinning to the floor.

Pino and Somers plunged over him and grappled Farr together. Dazed, paralyzed, Frank John saw the marshal running, gun in hand; Patterson and the sheriff beyond him, charging down; Jim, the saloonkeeper, heaving up a chair to strike. Lewis leaped forward, Johnny Pardee behind, Frank John one second later. That made him too late. In that blink of time, before he could even overtake the crippled Pardee, it was all over. Lewis caught up the saloonkeeper and hurled him crashing. Farr broke loose from Pino and struck Somers in the face. A streak that was Bill Hawkins left his chair. He hurled his muscular body through the air in a perfect football tackle, caught Farr around the knees and brought him down, dragging Somers with him. Hawkins made a convulsive scramble and fell on Farr's chest and his one free arm. Simultaneously, Lewis sat on Farr's legs. Hawkins smiled up at the marshal and lifted a hand, palm out.

'I got him for you,' he said. 'Want me to help you lead him to jail?'

Quick work. Salt had not yet had time to get to his feet. The sheriff and Patterson, with only twenty feet to travel, were still too late.

'Get up, you!' said the marshal. 'Will you come peaceable or do we put the handcuffs on you?'

'Lemme think it over,' said Farr dispassionately.

He sat up, inspected the wreck that had been his shirt, and reached for his hat. At last he came to a decision. 'Oh, peash'ble, I guess. Help me up, shomebody.'

'Take his other arm, Hawkins,' said the marshal. 'Sheriff, can't you and Erie go down to the judge's house before he turns in? I want to consult with him and you. I'll be down as soon as I get Farr tucked into bed.'

'Well, that's over,' said Johnny. 'Pres, I'll get a bottle and we'll go up to my room, where it's quiet. Come on, Frank John. But we'll have some coffee and pie first, steak and eggs and a few little fixin's. I haven't had a thing to eat since supper. Pres pays.'

Johnny pulled off his boots, not without a groaning, and stretched himself on the bed. As a medicinal measure, Johnny was using for his injury the popular New Mexican panacea of letting nature take her course. The two guests selected the best and only chairs.

'Well,' said Frank John, explosively indignant, 'are you going to let your friend go to jail? Can't you bail him out?'

'Best place for him,' said Johnny heartlessly. 'He'll be sobered up by morning. He certainly is one plumb pest when he's full. Sad about Jack.

Sober, he could clean out that whole bunch. But when he's sober there's no fight. It's too blamed bad.'

'And as if three to one wasn't odds enough against him,' cried the boy bitterly, 'that big lubber of a Hawkins had to make a fourth—to curry favor with the officers, I suppose.'

Lewis and Pardee exchanged glances. There was laughter in their eyes. But when Frank John looked his way, the Lewis eyes were filmed and dreamy.

'The brave boy seized the brawny Indian and hurled him over the beetling precipice into the seething waves below,' Pres murmured joyfully, groping in the dead past. Then he turned his head, blinked, and came back reluctantly to the present. ''Enry was just in time to keep the marshal from shooting Farr,' he explained. 'If 'Enry jumps the marshal, Tinhorn Jim beats Farr's brains out with that chair—so far as 'Enry knows. So 'Enry 'Awkins, he has just one finger snap of time to decide and do. He downed Farr. Good man, 'Enry. I warm my hands at him.'

'What? You mean Hawkins was on Farr's side?'

'Just that. Otherwise, old Elmer was due to stop a bullet.'

'You don't think the marshal meant murder?' demanded Frank John, horrified.

'Then why the gun? He didn't need no gun to make the arrest,' said Johnny. 'Sheriff didn't pull his gun—notice that, Pres? We'll have to remember that, come settling day. And the Rockingchair boys are not so bad either—not when you stack 'em up beside the Ladders. Coming back to the murder, Frank John; the sheriff didn't mean murder, but the marshal did. Jim Yewell had the inclination and the opportunity. Jack Farr talked like a fool, was bound to start a row, did start a row. He was a stumbling block to Yewell and his gang. And what Farr said was true, every word. Target is no place at all, just because there's an organized gang of crooks here, running wild. What I don't see is why the good men don't get together and clean up Gridiron so it will be fit to live in.'

'Really good men, they never do much of anything—not when it's risky,' said Pres. 'Always fussing about the rules, stopping for Sunday and advice of counsel. Then, they foster a brutal prejudice against guessing, good men do. Worst of all, they wonder does it pay. That's fatal—that last. What you want is a few trusty knaves. Let's count. Elmer, the sot, the trouble hunter. No question about Elmer. Johnny, the cowman. That's two. Passing on with averted heads, hastily but kindly, I'm the next.'

Frank John laughed.

'Do you doubt my rascality, then? When you've seen with your own eyes?' demanded Pres indignantly. 'You see me drink and gamble and cheat in a poker game. You saw me make the fifth to jump on one poor drunken donkey in a barroom row——'

'Rats! You just caught hold of Farr's legs to square yourself for standing the saloonkeeper on his head,' said Frank John, shrewdly enough. 'If the sheriff had seen fit to call you to account, you would have claimed you thought Jim Gem was siding with Farr.'

'It did answer a lot of questions, me hopping his hump that way,' said Pres dryly. 'And it certainly didn't hurt Farr any. That idea may have occurred to me. And so, Frank John, according to your own say, I'm a liar, too—or would have been if the sheriff had seen fit. As a matter of fact, however, mighty few sheriffs ever do see fit,' said Pres dreamily. 'They never did see fit. It's a habit with them. Now we'll tally up—gambler, cheat, liar and bully. Oh, I qualify, all right. That's three. And 'Enry 'Awkins makes Number Four.'

'Come! I say! Five minutes ago Hawkins was a good man, and who so loud to praise him as you?'

'I may have used the words,' Pres admitted. 'But it is barely possible that "good man" doesn't mean here just what it does in Maryland and Michigan.'

'A good man means generous, loyal and brave,' said Frank John hotly. 'Here or in hell!'

Lewis went on placidly, ignoring the interruption: 'Mistrusted 'Enry from the start. Too quiet. Fine, big, broad-shouldered man, inconspicuous, melted into the landscape like a quail. Hiring a bronc' broke, and him bow-legged as a pair of tongs. Walks on the right-hand side, no matter who he's walkin' with. Shooting that poor devil of a horse——'

'Oh, was that who it was?'

'——to save Johnny's worthless hide, and doing it without any gun that anybody saw. And that makes another lie I told. Four knaves. You are the fifth, Frank John. Take off your coat and pitch in, but keep your shirt on.'

'Me? What have I done?' Frank John blushed with not-unbecoming confusion. It was plain he took the charge of knavery as an unmerited accolade. 'And what use could I be to your league of rogues?'

Unspoken, a half-forgotten line flashed through his mind. Where had he read that, or heard it? Oxford, Carlisle, The Highlands, Normandy, Avignon? '*We are the lost. Queen Honor*——' How did it go? ... '*Queen Honor is the deathless*——' Who had said that? How could he have forgotten? ... '*A battered rascal guard still closes round her.'* . . . His blood tingled hot and proud; it flushed his boyish face with pleasure.

'As for your first asking, son—well, for one thing, you keep mighty bad company,' said Pres. 'And for the other point, you don't seem to realize that you'd be simply invaluable to us. You could go around asking questions when, if we'd do the like, we would never see sundown. Besides, we could explain things to you——'

'Oh, I know! You could explain, so you'd know what you meant yourself. You don't know that most of the time. You act by instinct, mostly, like the other wild animals. And by the time you spelled it out so I could get a glimmer, the rest would have it down like a plain, straight road so that the wayfaring man may not err therein. Thank you most to pieces, but I'm going home.'

'Don't think of such a silly thing. That would be rank wasteful. Quite aside from the civic service you can up and go and do in this blessed emergency, you want to consider your education. You don't appreciate your opportunities, Frank John. You have a fine inquiring mind; and you want to remember that in a thousand years, or some such, historians will publicly offer their right eye to know what you can see now, at first-hand; just as they puzzle and stew and guess about Harold the Saxon, nowadays. Ain't people funny? Heavens to Betsy, how they'd raise the roof, them sharps, if they could lay hands on a few anecdotes by Little John, in his own handwrite, about Robin Hood and the proud Sheriff of Nottingham! But if they'd found those same letters while Little John was alive, they would have lit the kitchen fire with 'em. Ain't that queer? Well, you take warning by that, and keep your eyes open. Here you are, living in the ancient days and the springtime of the world, with a priceless chance to get the low-down on how we scramble through with a certain cheerfulness and something not far removed from decency, and make merry with small cause. You stick around, Frank John, and watch our ways and means. . . . Besides, we need you.'

'No, I thank you! I'm not taking any. I'd only be a clog on you. I don't fit in here. I don't see closely enough, I don't think quickly enough, and I don't move quickly enough. Target is no place at all for me. I'm going back home. As John Cecil Calvert, among his own people, I can pass muster. Not here.'

So, in humility and all good faith, John Cecil Calvert spoke his mind. It was his last recorded utterance—as John Cecil Calvert. Today, when New Mexicans would boast, they point to Frank John, pillar and landmark, name giver. It was he who gave to the Blue Bedroom that beloved name; incidentally, for many old-timers, Frank John was their only approach to the treasures of the English tongue.

Frank John did not go back home. For, as he rose to go, a discreet tapping came at the door. Frank John opened it. Hawkins stood framed there, upstanding, alert and tall, his face alight, his eyes dancing, finger on lip. He stepped in and closed the door softly.

CHAPTER VIII

IT WAS ONLY four blocks to the jail, two east and two south. It was a leisurely saunter. The prisoner draped one affectionate arm on the marshal's shoulder, held fast the Hawkins coat sleeve with the other hand, and chatted brightly of night and stars and the fishes of the deep; bidding them a cheery good-night as Knowles, the jailer, ushered him to a cell.

'Mr. Hawkins, will you stop in at Judge Humphries' place with me?' said the marshal as they turned back. He spoke in undertones.

'What for? I was thinking some of bed.'

'Got a proposition to make to you. . . . What's the matter? What are you stoppin' for?' The marshal turned his head for the last words. Hawkins had halted in his tracks.

'You got no square business to spring on me in the middle of the night,' said Hawkins bluntly. 'Look here, Yewell; this looks like some shenanigan.'

'Sh-h-h! Not so loud. Shenanigan? Why, yes, it

is, in a way. But it is only a necessary stratagem of the law. We want your help—the sheriff and Erie and me,' said Yewell. 'We was considerin' you for the job this afternoon, mainly because you and Dave Salt tangled up. On account of that, nobody would think of you pulling a job for our crowd. Seein' the way you arose and shone durin' the recent ruckus with Farr, we could hardly do better. You're not squeamish, I judge.'

Mr. Hawkins nibbled at the edges of this remark, wide-eyed and alert. Under his wide hat, his face was undecipherable in the starlight, but his voice was harsh:

'Why at the judge's? Why not at the hotel? Listen, fellow; I don't go into anything blind. Give it a name.'

'Here on the street? Think I'm crazy? That's why we go to the judge's, and why we go in the dark. It's a night job, and tonight is the night.'

'You give it a name,' said Hawkins stubbornly. 'I can always say no and go home to bed, if I don't like it. I dance for no man's piping, unless I call the tune.'

'Conscience ache ye?' sneered Yewell. 'Well, all I got to say is, you don't look it.'

'Give it a name,' said Hawkins. 'This is the third and last time. Tell it to me!'

'There's houses along here. Want everybody to hear us? Vacant lot down the street a ways. Tell you there.' He strode on through the starlight. Hawkins followed him a step behind.

Thrifty cottonwoods lined the street before the vacant lot. In the dark shadows the marshal stopped and spoke in an angry whisper:

'It's the Carmody outfit. They're camped out of town a ways and they shoved their little old horse herd over the ridge, a mile or so farther on, where the grass is better. We want you to run off that horse herd. Not steal 'em, just chase 'em off to the mountains any which way, and as much farther as you see fit. Then you can leave them and double back by some different route. Tell you why, up to the house, but that's all we want you to do. Month's pay for one night's work. Half a night—'twill be midnight by the time you get your horse and get started.'

'Shucks, is that all? I thought, by the way you was taking on, you wanted me to hide a train of cars in a well, or burn somebody in bed. But why to-night? Why not tomorrow night, so I could scatter 'em and get back before day and no one the wiser? The way you've got it framed out, I'll be suspected.'

'And you act like a cowman, too,' said Yewell, irritated. 'Don't you see, their cattle are dog-tired, so they couldn't get 'em farther out this evening, waterin' as late as they did? Tomorrow they'll water at noon and shove the herd 'way out to good grass, and the horse herd will be right beside the bed ground. It's tonight or never. Come on, let's go talk it up.'

'But why go up to the house?' asked Hawkins. 'Why don't I go on from here? I don't care to have everybody know my business. Why take all Target in on the deal?'

'You're the most cautious man I ever saw! Why, there's nobody there but the sheriff and Erie and the judge; and we're all in it. Four heads are better than one, and we don't want to overlook any bets. This has to come off as slick as grease. Give you instructions after we consider every angle. Got to get your money, too. And I want you to be sure the law is back of you, so you won't get scary and spoil it all,' said the marshal with an ill-concealed sneer. 'Most suspicious fool I ever did see. Come on, we're wasting time.'

The judge's house was set back from the street. Francis Truesdale Humphries had not favored adobe. He was from New Hampshire, and his house was of wood, weatherboarded, painted white, with green facings. In memory of other skies, the house perched upon stilts, boarded up to the hollow semblance of a basement. The large front room served as office; behind was a bedroom, with a kitchen beyond, which was also the dining room. The judge was unmarried. Hawkins remembered the place from daylight, because it was so unlike its neighbors. The back yard was surrounded by a high board fence. There, in earlier days, Humphries had raised chickens, to the great joy of Target. The far-flung New England conscience—or perhaps a habit—drove him to keep it whitewashed still. In the rear of this yard, flush with the alley, stood the abandoned chicken house, now falling to decay; flanked by a shed which was meant to stable one horse, before the judge had learned the good old New Mexico method of keeping horses; which is to turn your horse loose on the flat. Then, when you wanted to go somewhere, you could walk or wait till your horse came in for water.

The judge's curtains were drawn, but lines of light streamed out at the edge to show the tiny lawn. The graveled walk was neatly bordered by beer bottles set on end, necks down; a clipped lilac centered the lawn, and morning-glories latticed the covered porch.

The marshal tapped and entered. The sheriff looked like a tired man—which he was—a heavy man, sullen and slow and slightly bewildered, a man on whom the years were telling. He had thrown hat, coat and gun on a settle by the door, and was now sprawled on a sofa near the unlit fireplace, his boots toppled together for mutual support where he had kicked them off. He sat up grudgingly as Patterson and Judge Humphries rose to greet the newcomer. Erie Patterson was cordial and frank in his welcome. The judge was fluttered.

'Well, here's your Hawkins,' announced the marshal. 'Judge, you are the very spit and image of respectability, safety, and all that. You take this geezer in hand and reason with him. Most uneasy critter I ever did see. I've known a lady to leave her happy home for less persuasion. Sit up, Hawkins. You're among friends.'

'I done heard about that lady,' said Hawkins, smiling. 'Heard it on night guard.' He crooned softly, with no unpleasant voice:

Oh, would you leave your home and would you leave your baby,
And would you leave your own true love for to go with Black Jack Davy?

'The answer is, I will.' So saying, he sank on the settle and looked up inquiringly at Judge Humphries.

'My dear fellow,' said the judge, 'it's quite simple. We want to know more about the Carmody outfit. But if the sheriff or anybody else goes prowling around them, they'll be suspicious and we'll learn nothing. The more so as there has been some unfortunate friction between them and Erie's men, as I hear. There is where you come in. No risk at all, since you act at the behest of the law. You are to run their horses off and scatter them. They will come to us with their complaints; the sheriff and Mr. Yewell will raise a posse, find the horses, and so become friendly and intimate with them at their own asking.'

'The fact is,' said Erie Patterson, watching Hawkins and glimpsing incredulity behind his attentive eye—'and this is the strictest confidence, mind you—the fact is, we suspect Carmody of some knowledge—if indeed it goes no further than that—of this man Bill Doolin.'

'The outlaw? Is that the way the land lies?' cried Hawkins eagerly. He eyed his informant shrewdly. So doing, he heard, slight but distinct, the faint protest of a chair in the next room, the shuffle of a cautious foot. Greed showed in his eyes as he went on, 'There'll be a reward for his capture or safe burial, I'm hearing?'

'There is, indeed,' said Erie, smiling. 'It is that reward which stirs us up. Naturally, no suspicion must fall on us about this horse herd. We are all going back up to be in evidence in the saloon just as soon as you start.'

'I'm not,' said the sheriff shortly. 'I'm going to bed, right here and soon.'

'Well, the rest of us are going,' said Erie. 'My reputation is none so good but what an alibi is welcome. The rest of our boys are there now, lapping it up. There's where you come in, Mr. Hawkins. This Carmody man will snoop around and inquire about our crowd the first thing.'

'I'm the very man you want!' said Hawkins, flushing with enthusiasm. 'I hung back a bit at first. It looked fishy to me, and that's a fact. But I'm with you now. All I hope is that it isn't a false alarm. I'd like to finger some small slice of that reward money.'

'Carmody and Doolin are old friends; we're dead sure of that much,' said the marshal, and Hawkins turned trustful eyes upon him. 'Our thought, and hope, is that Doolin keeps in touch with him. Hides out in the hills, but comes in by night for supplies and information. You notice all tracks, will you?'

Hawkins' face fell and lengthened; the eager light fled from his eyes. 'What if this devil, Doolin, was to catch me in my little enterprise during the course of his night prowling? Where would my month's pay be then? "No risk at all!" says you.

I'd call it one hell of a risk. Too much for that money. I might have known it. Easy money is the hardest, always.'

'Pshaw! There's no danger. Doolin would have no business at the horse herd. Why should he? He might be at the wagon, but it is the wagon you must shun. You know where they're camped?' Hawkins nodded. 'Give him his money, Erie. Pay him double. This has got to be done tonight, remember.'

Erie slid three double eagles into a waiting hand. But Hawkins looked at the golden tokens without satisfaction. 'Say, I'm a top hand,' he said. 'I don't work for no thirty a month. But I'll tell you what I'll do. I've got a good rifle over in the feed corral, with my saddle. But on such a chancy business as this, in the dark, a six-shooter beats any rifle. Give me a good six-shooter and I'm your man.'

'In the devil's name, take that six-shooter layin' there by you and get out of here!' said the sheriff. 'It'll be morning before you get started, and I got a jail full of guns. You take the horses to the foothills of San Lorenzo before daylight, and I don't care if you never come back!'

'Oh, I'll be back,' said Hawkins. 'I'm interested in Bill Doolin and that reward money. Nuff talk. 'Night, everybody!' He took up gun belt and gun, and buckled the belt on as he went down the walk.

He crossed the street diagonally, walking briskly. At the street corner, close at hand, he turned north toward the feed corral, where his horse was. But he did not go there. He went north one block, east one block, turned south one block, stopping at the corner, peering cautiously to make sure that the judge's street was deserted; crossed the judge's street, turned down the judge's alley, slinking in the shadows, noiseless. He was delayed somewhat at the door of the judge's one-horse stable, which was hooked inside; lifted the hook with a poking gun barrel, fastened it behind him, crept like a ghost through the judge's garden, crawled without sound in a shadowed detour, and wormed himself under the kitchen, into the false basement beneath the judge's house. Slowly, with infinite caution, he came snakewise under the front room. There were holes in the floor and thrusting shafts of light and the sound of many voices.

'All right, boys!' said the marshal. He had been watching Hawkins from below a lifted corner of curtain; he rose now and dusted his knees.

The bedroom door opened and three men tramped out, blinking in the sudden change from darkness to light—Dave Salt; Nash, the grocer; Ellis Kames, the lawyer.

'Where's that bottle?' demanded Salt savagely. 'Thought you was going to keep up that yap all night. Where's your glasses, judge?'

'In that wall cupboard. Help yourself; you're up on your hind legs.'

'I thought I would have to sneeze in spite of everything. I'm next with that bottle, Dave.' Thus Nash for Cash, Groceries.

'It hands me a laugh to think of that poor boob, and what a surprise he's going to get,' said Ellis Kames, darkly handsome, faultlessly attired, as attire went in that day—a Prince Albert coat, a black string tie, a glossy black hat.

'He was a shy fish,' said Yewell. 'Shy, but greedy. Only for that reward he might have backed out. Then where would your fine plan have been, Ellis?'

'Then I would have hatched another plan. I concocted this one, you will do me the justice to observe, in some haste, owing to your joint desire to involve Carmody and get the B 4 cattle at forced sale. I rather plume myself on that plan, for an impromptu. "An excellent plot, very good friends."'

The allusion was lost. 'Too many if's and and's,' growled the sheriff. 'Something will slip up on you. The old army game is the surest and safest.'

'In many ways I quite agree with you, Steve,' said Ellis Kames tranquilly. . . . 'If you are quite done with that bottle, Nash? . . . Thanks.' He poured a stiff drink, tossed it off, passed the bottle, and wiped his mustache delicately with a bordered kerchief. 'The bank money is ours, certainly, any time we choose to take it. Personally, I believe we might get more by waiting longer—although I may be in error. This is not a rich country, and there is not much loose money that is not already on deposit here. But this scheme works both ways. We get the cash and Carmody gets in bad. Other things being equal, I would cast my vote for this lay, just to see that white-livered boob of a Hawkins buried as Bill Doolin. That hands me a laugh!'

'Simplest way is the best way,' said the sheriff stubbornly. 'This has to run like a time-table. And you know how often trains are late.'

'Let's go over it, then, to make sure it works like a time-table. Everybody set your watches together before we leave. Bank opens at nine. Somers is in the bar, setting 'em up, to make sure everybody's in off the street. Salt has a smoky horse, in the side street —a horse which looks very much like the Hawkins horse. He's dressed just like Hawkins, with a floppy black hat like Hawkins wears. Salt, as everyone knows, bought him a new pearl-gray hat last night, on account of an accident to his old one. There we are—nine o'clock, street empty. Salt's watching.

Now comes my part. I go into the bank, make a deposit, come out when the bank's empty and go in the saloon, where I am drinking deep when the robbery occurs. That gives Salt the tip. He puts on his little old mask, slips in and holds up the flaxy cashier, puts the money in a meal sack and hops his horse. He rides down that street to the alley, sees the sheriff a block down the street, walking his way, bringing friend Farr up from jail to stand trial. So the bold bandit whirls into the alley across from the bank. Farr sees that, and can swear to it. . . . Get that, Salt?'

Salt scowled. 'What's the idea? You taking all that pains to be sure the sheriff will be coming down the street at just that exact minute. Kames, are you insinuating that I might doublecross my friends and light out with all of it?'

'My dear Dave! What an idea! You pain me, you do indeed. That was to have Farr—no friend of ours—able to swear the robber went down the alley. That you couldn't ride down the street and over the hills to Mexico, because Steve would shoot your eye out and earn high praise as an efficient peace officer, in case your evil spirit prompted you not to turn down that alley, as per schedule—that is just a coincidence.'

'To hell with all of you,' snarled Salt. 'Let someone else pull your chestnuts from the fire. I won't.'

'There, there,' said Erie. 'You shan't do it if you don't want to. But I think you might, Davy. You're the only one of us as big as Hawkins, and Hawkins, he's just about Bill Doolin's size, from all accounts, and we might get that reward, being this is a hot country and all. Bank robber tracked up and killed resisting—had to bury him—Doolin seen and positively identified near by, only a week ago; suspicious actions of the man Carmody, supposed to have been Doolin's confederate—why, it's a fair cinch! And the real Doolin won't be seen again—not if he hears of it. That will be his chance, and he'll be smart enough to take it. He's married, and he'd quit—so I hear—if the officers would let up on him—as they would, if they thought he was dead. That five thousand would help, Dave, if you felt like going through with it. Never mind Kames; he always has to have his little joke.' Erie's voice was honeyed, almost cooing. 'You think it over, and do whatever you think best. But I think you might go on with it, Dave, so long as none of the rest of us can fill the bill. Look at what I have in my hand, Dave. Don't you think you might go on with it?'

What Patterson had in his hand was cocked, and the muzzle was so adjusted as to cover a point just above Dave's belt buckle. Dave thought he might go on with his part, and said so, while sweat rolled into his eyes.

'Another little joke of mine, friend Dave,' remarked Kames, 'is that Jim Yewell will be at the back door of the saloon at just that exact minute—as you so aptly phrased it—just to make sure that your evil spirit doesn't turn you up the wrong alley. As a further coincidence, Newt Somers will stand at the end of the bar, next to the front door, and that door opened. I am a poor shot myself,' said the lawyer apologetically, 'but Newt is considered well above the average, I believe. And since Bart Pino will be sitting on the judge's porch at that exact minute, cleaning the judge's rifle for him—really, it would seem that the robber must infallibly be shot, unless indeed he turned up the alley back of the Nash for Cash grocery store. Cheer up, Dave. Your part is nearly over. You only have to carry that money a hundred and fifty feet, be the same more or less. Then a quick dash, and you're in the clear. . . . Your turn, Erie. Speak your piece.'

'At nine sharp, Nash and I are in his office at the rear of the store—just the two of us. Nash has a brown leather valise, neither new nor old, unnoticeable. The valise is open. I have a double-barreled shotgun. The shotgun is loaded. Buckshot, I believe. There is a back door in the office, leading to the alley. The door is open. I stand by the back door with the shotgun. As Dave races by, he throws the sackful of money—if I remember rightly—through the open door. That's right, isn't it, Dave?'

Dave confirmed this.

'We all want to be letter-perfect in our parts,' observed Patterson pleasantly, 'so that everything will go off smoothly. To resume: Dave throws the sack into us at the open door; we dump the money into the satchel; Nash locks the satchel, giving me the key to the satchel; we pop the satchel in the safe, we turn the combination, we dispose of the meal sack—ordinary meal sack; fifty like it in Nash's lumber room. Questioned, however, it appears that the back door was shut and not open. Mr. Nash and I did not see the robber pass, but we heard a horse running. We opened the door and looked, just in time to see a man and a horse turn out of the alley into the street—the street just beyond the judge's house. That's all we know.'

'You confirm this, Mr. Nash?'

'That's how it was,' said Nash. 'Horse was running as hard as he could go. Couldn't see its color for the dust. . . . And the money is safe in the safe.'

'Safe in the safe!' Kames repeated. 'Safe, because friend Nash has too much property to leave. Not to mention the enormous line carried in his store—and paid for, gentlemen, as I made it my business to ascertain—paid for, except for a few recent invoices. Aside from that, Nash owns real estate and a substantial block of stock in the Railroad cattle ranches. We may be quite sure that Mr. Nash will never contemplate other than a fair and equitable division of the spoil. So much for that. The money is safe; and now we must see to it that Dave Salt is safe. He has borne the burden and heat of the day; he has taken more risk than any other—oh, far more risk! He is to have a double share for his pains, and he is to have an unbreakable alibi. He throws the money into Nash's office, as related. Then, and not till then, Dave goes on full tilt up the alley, unmolested, as fast as his horse can run, till he comes to the door of the Humphries stable. That door is open. He rides in and jumps off; he closes the door and hooks it from within. Bart Pino is in the stable, and Bart Pino's new saddle, creaking new, with silver conchas, gaudy Navajo blanket and a bridle to match, is in the stable.

'Bart strips off the shabby old saddle and bridle—the judge's, long disused, unnoticeable—and replaces it with his own beautiful rig. With a gentle horse the change can be made in one minute by a man in haste. This is a gentle horse, and Bart has reasons for haste. Let us now go back to Dave.

Jumping off, Dave runs to the front of the back yard, where his own horse stands, ready saddled with Dave's own saddle, well known to everyone. Judge Humphries awaits him there with Dave's new hat—the one he is wearing now. He takes from Dave the old, black, floppy hat—Dave has already dropped his mask in the alley. The high board fence hides all these hurried transactions. Bart joins Dave there; they lead their horses through the gate to the front of the judge's house; the judge has gone in with the floppy black hat. The alarm is given. Dave and Bart proceed down the street, the judge accompanying them afoot, chatting together. To be sure, Bartolome Pino is riding a smoke-colored horse. That is nothing. There are many such horses. The bandit was an American and his saddle was old. This smoky horse is appareled like the sun and ridden by a Mexican with irreproachable companions, who will vouch for him if questioned. No man will think twice of the smoky horse. . . . Go on, judge; tell us what you know about this case.'

'Well, after breakfast I was cleaning my rifle, and when I went to put it together it wouldn't fit. So Dave and Pino was riding by and I asked them to help me. What time? Oh, half-past eight, or some such matter—I didn't notice. They was there 'bout half an hour on my front porch, Bart tinkering with my rifle and Dave fixing him a hackamore. Their horses? They tied 'em back of the house, seems like. Yes, they went back for 'em when we heard the hue and cry, because I was quite a ways up the street before they overtook me. Did I see anybody that might have been the robber? Come to think of it, I did see somebody, two or three blocks down, crossing the street and riding pretty fast. Didn't notice him particular. Why should I? Except that he seemed to be in a hurry. Riding north, he was. Come to think of it, I believe he had a black hat, this fellow. I couldn't be absolutely sure of that, but I seem to remember it that way. This was a big man, you say? I swan I don't know whether this fellow I saw was big or not. He was kinder humped over, I noticed.'

'That's the lay,' said Kames. 'See any flaws in it, anybody? The ayes have it. The rest is simple and governed by circumstances. We'll make up a posse and scour the country. More accurately, the authorities will do this. I'm not up to hard riding myself, as you all know. Carmody will miss his horses by sunup or before. He'll think they're just drifted, and hunt for them. It is not at all likely that he'll make a report before nine. Possibly not at all. If he comes, or sends word, the sheriff details a bunch to go with him and follow up the tracks. They'll find the horse herd, and they'll be sure to find the track where Hawkins rode off alone, because someone will be along who knows there'll be such a track.'

'I'll be one,' said Yewell, interrupting. 'Me and Erie go with the horse-trailing bunch; taking along a few outsiders for the looks of it. We'll find that track and insist on following it up. If just us two goes alone, so much the better.'

'That's the idea. You overtake Hawkins, on a smoky horse, wearing a floppy hat. Maybe you meet him coming back. In either case he resists arrest and you have to kill him. You've got the bank robber, but not the money. Accomplice likely; although he may have hidden it. An accomplice? Who? Who is this Carmody, this stranger? Isn't it queer that his horse herd should be run off just then, and at no other time? If Carmody, or his man Bird, or both, are out ostensibly looking for their horses, doesn't that look as though they were in collusion with the robber, hiding the money for him? And if, by any lucky chance, Carmody comes up with a report of his missing horses before the bank robbery, then it's as plain as the nose on your face. He wanted to draw as many as possible on the sheriff's posse, looking for horse thieves, to give the bank robbers a break. Anybody can see that, when the horses are found, and not one missing. However, we can hardly expect that much luck. Carmody will hunt his own horses, probably. But if we don't hear from his camp before the posse starts, we'll ride out by his camp to make inquiries. Then we'll send a bunch to hunt the stolen horses. And the dead robber—is it possible that this is Doolin himself? It is possible. Same general description, anyhow. Sheriff hasn't got back yet. When he comes he can wire and see. But we'll have to bury this long lad right now. He ain't keeping any too good. They can always dig him up for identification. . . . Boys, this is good! It works like a watch. Any questions? No? . . . Oh, yes, one thing more. . . . Steve, didn't you remember hearing, a long time ago, that Bill Doolin and this Carmody was close friends?'

'I don't remember anything of the kind!' roared the sheriff. He arose and pounded violently on the table. His big red face fairly swelled with rage. 'And no other man is going to remember it. It's a dirty rotten deal all the way around, without that. Carmody's going to have his chance without any perjury from me. Why don't you leave Carmody out of it? He's got a family. I don't give a damn about Hawkins. Don't like him; never did—surly, black-muzzled swine. But if you try to hang it onto Carmody I hope you make a botch of the whole job. Know what I think? I think I'm going to stake

Carmody to enough to get him and his herd out of here. Kames, you leave Carmody out of this or I'll shoot you in the belly! Hear me?'

'Come on, boys; let's go uptown,' said Nash for Cash. 'You'll need slickers tomorrow. Some folks have rheumatism when a rain is coming on, but it works on the sheriff's conscience. I've seen him this way before. He always gets over it. . . . Coming, judge?'

'No, I'll stay here with Steve.'

'Good night, then.'

Mr. Hawkins began to wriggle out while the feet of the departing conspirators allowed him to make a comparatively speedy escape by covering any small noises he might make. He effected his retreat in short order as far as the alley, but was quite unable to hook the stable door behind him. He contented himself with propping it shut with a stone, confident that the habits of small boys would account for this small circumstance, should it be noticed. Two blocks away he paused to take stock. He was woefully begrimed and becobwebbed. He wiped his face with a handkerchief; he brushed his clothes with his hat, and then brushed the hat with the handkerchief. Then he scratched his nose and took counsel with himself in a guarded whisper:

'That sheriff? Kind of pitiful, isn't it, Bill? . . . H'm! That's odd too. If that clever marshal hadn't told me that Bill Doolin and this Carmody was old friends, I'd have turned him down, and that would have been the end of it. But that statement interested me—and so it was only the beginning! Lying,' said Bill Hawkins sagely, 'is a bad habit. . . . That Nash, too. I don't take to Nash, somehow. Rheumatism is no subject for joking.'

He looked up at the sky. The clock said twelve and past. He made his way swiftly to Holland House, listened in the hall, heard there a low humming of voices, and tapped on Pardee's door.

CHAPTER IX

WHEN Hawkins joined the conferees in Johnny Pardee's room Frank John could hardly recognize him; this supple light-foot had so little in common with the clumsy oaf of yesterday, humped and slouching. And then he remembered that twice before, in decisive action, this same Hawkins had been swifter than his eyes could follow. Frank John pondered this.

The scrutiny was mutual. The newcomer eyed Frank John doubtfully and with some perplexity. One Hawkins eyebrow shot up; the other, after some deliberation, followed slowly; and he bent an inquiring gaze on the other occupants of the now-crowded little room.

'The boy with the taffy-colored hair is all right, 'Enry,' said Pres Lewis, answering the unspoken query. 'He'll do to take along. A little lacking in experience, it may be, but something whispers in my ear that he has some on the way. What with one thing and you shining like a Japanese lantern on a Christmas tree, fairly oozin' information at every pore, I seem to hear afar ancestral voices prophesying war.' He transferred himself to the bed and waved his hand at the vacated chair. 'Sit down and relieve your mind, 'Enry. Frank John will stand hitched. Didn't you notice him bulging to battle a while ago, a little late, but headed the right way? When so softly you came tapping, just now, we was in the very act of offering him the keys of the city on a lordly dish.'

'Enry's doubtful face cleared with this assurance. 'This is no kid's play, but I'll take your word for him. And a chair is the last thing I need just now. Listen, Lewis, will you do my askings first and wait till later to find out why? If I stop to explain, it will be too late.'

'Adventures first; explanations take such a dreadful time,' murmured Lewis, nursing his hands between his knees. 'Next room on one side is mine; Frank John's on the other. Nobody in them. Shoot!'

'Yes, and my empty room across the hall. For all that, I'm closing the window, if we smother,' said Hawkins. 'Eavesdropping has happened, to my certain knowledge.' He lowered his voice to the key of caution. 'Here's the lay: You come with me and wait at the far corner of the plaza. I'll get my horse from Gray's corral. Then you ride your prettiest out to Carmody's wagon and carry a message for me.

I'll wait here for you, and when you get back, us four will go into executive session and I'll tell you all about why.'

'What's the message?'

'I'll tell you the odds and ends as we go, but the main items must be written, or they wouldn't believe in them, and you a stranger. The fact is, when I bull-dogged our drunk a while ago, I plumb won the young affections of both money and brains, and they propositioned me to do dirt for 'em, cash in advance, right off. With hints of more to follow. First chore was to run off the B 4 horse herd.' Here Johnny made comment, but 'Enry held up his hand. 'No questions. Tell you later. Going on one o'clock right now. I'm delegatin' the job to Carmody's man, Charlie Bird. He must be off and gone as quick as he can. It's my job and I'm supposed to be well on the way.'

'Carmody must have a heap of confidence in you,' said Johnny.

'Never saw the man in my life till I bought a horse of him yesterday evenin'. But Charlie, he'll do what I tell him, and the old man will do what Charlie tells him. So that's all right.' Hawkins turned to Frank John: 'You got paper and pencil? Well and good; write what I tell you.'

So Frank John sat by a little table and wrote from dictation, as follows:

Friend Charlie: You and Carmody do just like I say, without wasting a minute. Don't fail. Don't make any move different to what I tell you. Important. I am banking on you. One, put your saddle on this horse of mine. Two, send me another horse by bearer, as good as this one, or as good as you got. Three, you take this horse and push your horse herd out to the San Lorenzo Mountain, right off, just as fast as you can. That's the big mountain, due north. I am supposed to do this, paid for it. And you got no time to waste. Four, tell Carmody not to make no report in the morning. When somebody comes he is to say the horses drifted and you went after them about sunrise, that you'll get 'em. Act like he wasn't a mite uneasy—which he needn't be. Five, about ten in the morning, or a little later, you catch you another horse and drift your horse herd back, but leave my horse behind to be found and wondered at. Better push him on a couple of miles beyond your herd, and then you hustle right back and move your herd before he can get with them. If you meet anyone, make your story match the one Carmody is to tell. You didn't see my horse or anyone like me. But for everything else you see, tell it straight and careless. Your horses drifted; you didn't think they'd do the like of that; you'll hobble them tonight. The bearer, Mr. Lewis, is all right. He cannot tell you the why of this, because I have not had time to tell him yet.

Charlie, I seen you yesterday at the stock pens, but I dodged you. So long.

'That's all. Here; I'll sign it,' said Hawkins. He took the pencil and traced an extravagantly wide capital S, an inch high, crossing it with two long, perpendicular lines; the whole making a firm and exceedingly plump dollar mark.

'That was the brand me and Charlie Bird planned to have together when we were boys,' said Hawkins, musing. 'Some folks are born with two strikes on them. . . . That's nonsense. That's doin' the baby act. It's not luck; it's the man. Every time. I had as good a chance as Charlie Bird did, every bit.'

'Charlie Bird?' said Frank John. His eyes were round with astonishment. 'That little dried-up manikin? He told me he had neither kith nor kin left alive. Poor, alone, hardly a shirt to his back, working for day wages and in all human probability not drawing even that; following a ruined and falling house. I don't see what Charlie Bird has that any man can envy.'

Hawkins folded the note and handed it to Pres Lewis. He lifted up his eyes and regarded Frank John attentively. 'Don't you?' he said, at last. 'Well, Mr. Lewis, we'll go get my horse.'

'Friend with the countersign,' said Hawkins, ten

minutes later, as he swung down from the smoky horse and handed the rein to Lewis. 'When you ride up to that camp, you ride a-whistlin', real loud and pleasant. That Charlie Bird, he's half Cherokee and half white, and them's two bad breeds. Don't know about Carmody, but from his tell yesterday, his patience is pretty well given out. You whistle. One or the other of 'em will be with the herd, and the other a-snoozin', so you'll have to step lively. It's all to the good that they don't know why, so they won't have nothin' to hide. But you hurry on back. I got a heap to tell you. Leave the new horse and my saddle with Gray till you call or send an order. But you bring my old rifle up to your friend's room.'

The program fell behind the schedule. It was later than two o'clock when the stolen horse herd, with the owner's right hand in charge, took the road for San Lorenzo. Haste though he might, it was half-past when Pres rejoined the conference room; finding there two young men of highly divergent pasts who were now wholly at one, each merely a mass of quivering curiosity; and Mr. 'Enry 'Awkins tranquilly asleep in his chair.

' "The time has come . . ." ' said Pres rather loudly, ' "to talk of many things ——" Hi! Don't shake him, Johnny. You donkey, you ought to know better than that. . . . 'Enry! Executive session! Up and tell us why.'

So 'Enry up and told them.

'But, Mr. Hawkins,' broke in Frank John, when the story came to where 'Enry had wormed his way under the house as reporter, 'you must have had a very strong hunch that the marshal was lying, to cause you to take such an extraordinary step as that.'

'I knew he was lying,' said Hawkins dryly. 'No guesswork about it. And it wasn't a step. I tell you I crawled on my belly like a snake, expectin' to bite a rattler any minute, over dead men's bones, and shiny what-are-yous, and ha'nts whisperin' "Boo" to me, and a cold skel'ton hand ketchin' me by the ankles. You gentlemen may not believe me, but I was glad to get out in the starlight again.'

The session was long. Hawkins' memory was excellent and he told the story with gusto and with excellent mimicry—plausible marshal, timid judge, complacent Kames, arrogant Patterson, baited Salt and the berserk sheriff. As he told of the system of checks and balances devised for the better guidance of Dave Salt, Hawkins paused for meditation. A look of wonderment spread over his dark face.

'That's odd too,' he said. 'What an outlaw needs in his pardners is just what an honest man wants in his, no more and no less. J'ever think of that? They both want a man they can depend on, come hell or high water. Cowards, traitors, jellyfish—God hates 'em and the devil won't have 'em. This Dave Salt and his likes ain't worth a damn a dozen!'

The story was ended at last, and once more Frank John spoke out of turn, having much yet to learn: 'Splendid! And now you can send the whole bunch to the pen.'

'Who? Me?' said 'Enry 'Awkins, touching his own chest with an astonished forefinger. 'Me, a stranger; my word against Law and Order in person? Me, in a witness box, ownin' up to shameless eavesdroppin'? I guess not. We don't tell nothin' to nobody.'

'You set an ambuscade then? Take them in the act?' cried Frank John eagerly; and, in the painful silence that ensued, became aware that he had sinned greatly. It was a bad moment for the boy. Dating from that small point, Frank John began a chastened and unquestioning career.

'And catch Dave Salt, with his own pals shooting him up like a cullender? Damn likely. That's what the dirty dogs planned. If anybody happened to catch on to Dave and go to foggin' him, his own crowd would shoot him down themselves and be in the clear. "Works like a watch," says that lousy lawyer, braggin' and boastin', swelled up like a frog in a churn. Well, just because Mr. Kames thought he was smart enough to make his layout foolproof, hog-tight, bull-strong and horse-high, we'll let him pull his play. Then we'll pull ours, like I'm going to tell you; and we make high, low, Jick, Jack, Jill, Jinny and the game card.'

'Give us your powders,' said Pres.

They crowded around the little table. Slowly, painstakingly, with keenest foresight, Hawkins gave them their powders. Discussion followed—substitutions, elaboration, strengthening. Dawn sparkled in the east when Hawkins went tiptoe through the hall, bearing his boots and a blanket from his bed. He slipped softly up a half-forgotten stairway in the trunk room at the rear, opened a rusted door, and so came to the long-deserted roof of Lindauer Place—a roof that had once been Fort Lindauer, and famed.

Behind him Johnny Pardee drew a long face. 'And me with a game leg,' he groaned. 'Ain't that luck for you?' Then he brightened perceptibly. 'Say, Pres! Gayly the Troubadour, he's just about taken over your job as First Assistant Providence, hasn't he?'

'Who? 'Enry? My son, 'Enry is a great medicine man. He has covered every possible chance, I think.

And now to bed, the bilin' of us. It's half-past four this very now. I'm leaving word with the desk to wake us at eight. This will be one long, hard day for all and sundry.'

But Pres was mistaken. 'Enry had left at least one chance uncovered. To be Assistant Providence is not a desirable job.

'Enry woke shortly after sunrise, strove with all diligence to sleep again—and failed, much to his disgust. He sought to peer through the loopholes where once long rifles had beaten off Apache bands. He found two of every three given up to birds' nests, old or new; so quickly fades the glory of this world. Crouched and cautious, he made his rounds, peering out to the four corners of the world. Smoke curled from a hundred chimneys, dogs ran upon pressing errands, jaunty horsemen went to and fro, wagons were astir, a baby crowded from a window to see a man bareheaded below, who swung a lusty ax at the woodpile. He watched a breakfasting through near-by windows, a kiss snatched at a door. He saw, beyond the plaza, the night operator bringing in the switch lights, section hands trudging to meet the hour of seven, a grumbling engine at the water tank. He saw the B 4 herd, grazing fanwise from the bed ground. And upon every side, in town and out of it, in the sandy streets, on the low sandy slopes, by barrow pit or roadside, stray beer bottles sparkled in the low sun.

The Holland House gong called loud in air, but ham and eggs with hot coffee were not for 'Enry—doomed by a hard fate to be twenty miles away with an ill-gotten cavvyard of horses. After tedious eternities, private Pres came discreetly to the roof, shortly after eight, with smuggled sandwiches. He took back 'Enry's blankets, lest an overzealous chambermaid should remark upon their absence. The next eternity was shorter; and at long last, barely three minutes before nine by 'Enry's watch, Herman Lindauer came puffing up the steep stairs, with protesting brows in an astonished face. On his heels came Johnny Pardee.

'Sh-h! Keep your head down and your voice down,' said 'Enry.

'What is this?' said Lindauer, whose English was excellent except in stress and agitation. 'Pres Lewis says I must come with Johnny, that it is all right, that I must not disobey you the slightest. And what Pres Lewis says I do, every time, you betcha! But what goes on?'

'Look at the roof of that house across the alley from Nash's place,' said Johnny. 'Aurelio Sais is there with a double-barreled shotgun loaded with buckshot. That house belongs to some of Aurelio's *gente*. He is to stick his head up for you to see, just as the clock strikes nine; so you'll know he's in on the play. Aurelio, he's one of the best.'

'Keep your head down, Mr. Lindauer—look through that little loophole,' urged Hawkins. . . . 'No, this one here. It slopes the right way for you to see Aurelio. Don't look over the wall, whatever happens. If we're seen everything is ruined.'

Aurelio Sais popped up a flame-red head for brief inspection. 'I see him,' said Lindauer. 'Enry's hand made a brisk arc above the wall, an arc invisible from the street. Aurelio vanished. 'You I don't know,' said Lindauer, 'but Pres and Aurelio, with my life I trust them. . . . Why, who is that?'

A swift clatter of unseen feet below; a horse came partly into his field of vision, gathering speed, a smoke-colored horse, a rider in faded blue, a large man with a flop-brimmed black hat. A half horse and a half man; more he could not see, because of his angled loophole, until they whirled into the alley. The rider hurled a mealsack through the open door and thundered up the alley.

'Watch now!' said Johnny. 'He'll ride in the open door of Humphries' old stable. See him? I'm not looking through no porthole, so you may know we savvy what's going on. We're wise to the whole thing.' A shout came from the street in front, another answered. There was a swift tumult, the sound of running feet. 'Look down now. You'll see the sheriff looking up the alley in ten or twelve seconds —coming from the right, just too late to see which way the robber went. See him?'

'That robber was made up to look like me, you know,' said 'Enry. 'That's why you're here—so I can help you get your money back—me and Aurelio. Aurelio's not to show up.'

'The sheriff, I see him, pointing up the alley—waving, shouting,' wheezed Lindauer. 'Robber? A conspiracy, what? The bank?'

'Yes—and the sheriff is in it—Yewell—Patterson—others. Hold on to yourself. You don't lose a cent, and a new day comes to Target——' A roar of indistinguishable voices, thunder of frenzied feet, a howling mob about the sheriff, frantic, gesticulating.

'But, Johnny—if you knew beforehand? Why, then?'

'Your money is now in Nash's safe, and in no more danger than when it was in your own. Less. Nash is in the gang, and he is to keep the money till the dust blows over. You get every cent back an hour from now, or as soon as the posse gets started. When that money comes out of that safe you'll be the man that takes it out. Then we get them piecemeal, separated. There's the man to thank—Hawkins. He brought the whole rotten mess to light. Everything provided for. Good men to watch Nash's front door—Munro and Tolson. Aurelio guards the back.'

'What's that they're calling?' said Lindauer, trembling. His face went red and white.

'They're yellin' "Bill Doolin,"' answered Johnny contemptuously. 'They planned to blame it on him. It wasn't Doolin robbed your bank. It was your friends and neighbors. Yes, and your own directors, some of them. Well, go down and keep a stiff upper lip. All you have to do is not to tell any living soul one word of what we told you. Look as if you was scared! Try to make it natural. That's it—that's good. You got a right to look scared. Just help to get the posse started, quick as you can. Hurry, now; you're overdue.'

A dervish whirl of hubbub, confusion and madness in the street below, till the sheriff leaped into a wagon and his bull voice bellowed above the tumult:

'Keep still, everybody! Shut up, I say! Stop it, you fools! . . . Gray, we want every horse and saddle in your corral, no matter who they belong to. . . . Yewell, you line up all the riding men and have them dig up rifles—them that has 'em. . . . Patterson, you see that they're mounted—those that haven't horses of their own. . . . Lindauer, see that everybody has arms and ammunition and canteens. . . . Holl, put up everything in the shop for lunches. . . . Lewis, you run down to the other restaurants and commandeer all they got cooked, and tell 'em to keep on cooking till we leave. . . . Hollocher, go to Troy Ware's house and tell him to bring all his men that's in town. . . . Kames, you're no good on a horse. You and the judge take charge here while we're gone. I'll want you to send some wires for me —tell you presently. And you two read all telegrams that come for me, and send messengers after us if necessary. . . . Now, judge, what was that you was trying to tell us? You saw him? Where?'

'I saw somebody who might or might not have been the robber,' said the judge modestly. 'Going north like hell in a hand basket. Dave and Bart was both with me, but I don't know whether they saw him or not. I thought nothing of it at the time, of course. Not till we heard the yelling down here.'

'That's him, I guess,' said the sheriff. 'Where's Aurelio Sais and Munro? Find 'em, somebody. Tolson too. We want every fighting man in town.' He turned to Farr, his forgotten prisoner, who sat tranquilly on the curb and smoked a peaceful pipe, swinging a foot in careless happiness. 'Farr, that lets you in. Lets you out, rather.' He chuckled at his own joke.

Farr removed his pipe and twisted his head back to look. 'I guess not,' he said indignantly. 'Drunk and disorderly. Ten and ten. I pay no fine; so you can make it twenty. Who'll make it forty? Do I hear forty? It is going to be main hot today.... Glad I'm not out on the blisterin' flat.'

'Drop it, you old fool. You're on my posse.'

'I demand my rights as an American citizen,' said Farr stubbornly. 'I was drunk as a lord, and quarrelsome. By all good rights I ought to be in jail all the rest of this month, anyway. Fine business this is. Put you in jail for carrying a gun; yank you out of jail illegally, and force you to pack a gun about none of your business, and get shot all to hell! I guess not!'

'Stop this clowning, you crazy fool. You're losing priceless time for me. You have to serve on a posse when summoned.'

'And if I don't you can punish me, eh?' said Farr severely. 'Send me to jail? All right, here I am. Do you expect me to take myself down and lock myself up?'

Farr made this play from his own inexhaustible stock of deviltry. He was as yet quite uninformed as to the league of knaves and their private purposes.

A leaguer now interfered. This did not suit their book at all. They wanted Slim Jack Elmer on that posse.

'Oh, Jack, shut up!' said Johnny Pardee. 'A joke's a joke. Quit it! You're delayin' the posse, just as the sheriff says. Of course you're goin'. That was Bill Doolin that robbed this bank, and you don't want him to get away with a play like that. We'll be a laughingstock.'

More he might have said, but here, at last, he caught the prisoner's eye. Farr got that urgent message, literally, 'in the bat of an eye,' as the saying goes.

'Doolin, eh?' said Farr, with wakening interest. 'That's different. I supposed all the time it was Albert Garst. I'd sure hate to shoot Albert.'

'Double-damned fool!' growled the sheriff. 'All the same, I'd not be sorry to have old Elmer Farr at my back, if I was to meet up with Bill Doolin.'

'You've insulted me, Steve Davis,' said Farr. 'Your posse will split up and I'm not going with you. I'm going to be at Jim Yewell's back!' His face brightened with that thought. He rose to go, and sidled toward Yewell with a spreading and golden smile.

Yewell looked most unhappy at this suggestion. But Pres Lewis laughed loud and long, and slapped the marshal on the back. 'He's pulling your leg, Jim! He needs one drink to settle his tummy, and then he'll feel a heap better. You take me and Erie and Farr with you and we'll do our damnedest to get Doolin; just us four.'

'Doolin, hell!' said the sheriff. 'Where's that man Hawkins? I believe it was Hawkins. I saw him. He looked like Hawkins; he wore a black hat, and his horse looked just like the Hawkins horse.'

'That's so. Where is Hawkins?' said Lewis, and his face fell at the unwelcome thought. 'I haven't seen him either, come to think of it. Now what do you think about that? Oh, blast the luck!'

'Lon Gray says Hawkins got his horse and beat it between twelve and one,' said the saloon keeper.

'Shucks!' said the marshal. 'I bet that's who done it. And here I was banking on a split in that reward money for Doolin! Never mind; our bank will pay handsome for Hawkins, and we'll get him or bust a tug.'

'They will, if we get the money when we get Hawkins,' declared Erie Patterson soberly. 'But if he's managed to get rid of it some way, gentlemen, our bank is busted flat! Leastwise, all except what me and other unlucky guys has borrowed of 'em. I bet they wish now they had loaned us more. I wanted them to do that, too—but they turned me down. Say, Lewis —— Where's Lewis gone to, all of a sudden?'

Lewis had gone to Gray's corral, all of a sudden. A horrible and unforeseen thought had arisen before him. These people noticed brands. They would see the new B 4 horse he had brought up in the dead watches of the night. Questioned, Lon Gray would tell of that late coming; attention called, some would remember the Hawkins saddle—and then the fat would be in the fire for a fact! Fortunately Lon Gray was an old friend, and it is an untouchable and priceless privilege of integrity that it may do the questionable, unquestioned and unhindered. Sweating profusely, Lewis contrived to speak apart with Lon Gray. That B 4 horse and saddle must be hidden away when the unmounted came for the commandeered horses. Right as rain, said Lon Gray, and would Pres go peddle his papers, and stew no more about that horse?

Messengers rode headlong to warn the Pack-saddle, Cline, Carberry, Cat Knapp and the south. Telegrams went forth to rouse up east and west against the bandit; a wire went to Argentine to organize and move east behind the mountains to join Troy Ware's men on the Gato. The posse was organized with surprising swiftness, ready and wait-

W. H. D
Koerner

The posse—a goodly cavalcade

Courtesy Ruth Koerner Oliver

ing before Troy Ware and his retainers had arrived from Ware's town house to join them. Even then, three good men were not to be found—Aurelio Sais, Munro, Tolson. The sheriff would wait no longer, and departed, cursing those three by name. The posse rode north together, a goodly cavalcade, planning inquiry as to any glimpse of the fugitive at the Carmody herd before they separated to comb the country.

As prearranged, Lindauer came to the stairway, shortly after the posse had fairly started, and summoned the watcher to come down. But Hawkins called to the banker to come up on the roof instead, and waited there, despite Lindauer's fuming impatience, until he saw the posse gather around the B 4 wagon, linger there for a space, and then ride on—to separate beyond into three parties, spreading fanwise, north, northeast and nearly east. He noted with keen satisfaction that the smallest body rode northeast toward Staircase—five men, his sharp eyes assured him. Common sense had told them that the Ladder men would go east to search the Ladder range; that the largest body of men would go to comb the enormous bulk of San Lorenzo; that Troy Ware's men would go that way into their own country, passing beyond in due time to their northern range on the Feliz; that the sheriff would head them, the sooner to get in touch with the contingent which would be starting from Argentine. It was logical to suppose that the Staircase party would be headed by the marshal; that Pres, as a Staircase man familiar with the country, would be a second; that Farr, in accordance with his expressed determination, his recent wordy altercation with the sheriff, and the known bad feeling between himself and the Ladders, would make a third. It was 'Enry's hope that the marshal's distrust and fear of Farr, together with the influence of Lewis, would determine that Erie Patterson would be the fourth. This was probable; Lewis was a known man, his word listened to. Such a decision was the more likely, since the Ladders would pick up their foreman for leader—Curly Parker, a tried fighting man—and since Erie was next friend and crony to the marshal. As to the fifth, that was sure to be none other than Frank John, the disciple. Hawkins was a little surprised that one or two others had not been detailed with this party, but ascribed it to good management by Pres Lewis.

He came downstairs, highly elated. But he made a further delay in the dining room—chaperoned and vouched for by the banker—to absorb one steaming cup of coffee; which same he had sadly missed. They were joined there by Johnny Pardee, excused from active service for cause. Lindauer strictly enjoined the dining room to absolute silence as to Hawkins—whereat the dining room, in one collective bound, leaped nimbly to the not-unnatural conclusion that Hawkins was a secret-service man in the banker's employ—a luckless detective, since this robbing had been pulled off while he had been on other affairs. Guarding against another robbery of freight cars, the dining room rather thought, and so expressed itself, sagely enough, to kitchen and office. However, the hotel kept honorable silence as toward outsiders.

The streets were deserted, the remaining buzzers now buzzing in the saloon. So Lindauer, Hawkins and Johnny passed unnoticed into the street on their way to recover the stolen money and bear it back to its own proper home.

CHAPTER X

Mr. Ellis Kames sauntered across the Plaza from the freight depot, and idly flipped with a slender cane at pebbles in the path. Two small Mexican urchins played at marbles in that smoothly beaten path. They rose on their knees to yield the right of way. But Mr. Kames waved his hand airily and stepped aside, leaning on his cane to watch the game with smiling indulgence. From time to time he glanced about him, beaming upon the world with vague benevolence. A puff of smoke feathered and grew over the False Divide. Mr. Kames smiled. That was the Westbound Limited, toiling over Misery. That train was a short half hour away, was due to leave Target at ten-thirty-five. He took out a small pen-knife with a handle of glistening pearl, delicately cut the tip from the most crooked of all corkscrew cheroots, lit it, puffed with a cheerful satisfaction that was pleasant to see, glanced again at that low smoke in the east, flourished his cane in amiable salute to the marble players, and took up his loitering way.

The cane went gently tip-tap up the steps to the prosperous establishment of Nash for Cash. Mr. Kames turned in here. One customer stood at the counter. Kames waited idly until her small wants were filled; scanning the well-stocked shelves so absently that he didn't remark the customer's departure.

'Yes, Mr. Kames?' said the clerk at last.

'Ah, Walter,' said Kames, recalling his vagrant thoughts with an effort. 'Oh, yes! Mr. Nash is in the private office, I presume?' The cane lifted.

'Yes, sir. Shall I announce you, sir?'

'Oh, no, it is an appointment. Er—Walter, please do not let anyone disturb us.'

'I will see to it, sir.'

Kames glanced around the empty store, smiling faintly. 'I see that your fellow clerk—Churchill, is it?—was a member of the posse.'

'Yes, sir. Mr. Nash said he could spare one of us. And so,' said Walter, blushing, 'we tossed up a coin, and Churchill won.'

'Ah, youth, youth!' said Kames, smiling, with half a sigh. 'A sad blow to the community, this robbery.' He passed on languidly and opened the office door.

Nash jumped in his chair and rose with a flushed face. Kames smiled again, and seated himself, half standing, on the corner of Nash's low desk. 'My dear fellow,' said Kames pleasantly, 'you must learn to control your nerves. You are quite on edge.'

'You startled me.'

'Tut, tut, Charles! You invite suspicion. Sit down—sit down. Take it easy. My dear man, pattern yourself upon me. You have no cause for alarm. You were never safer in your life. Our little stroke of business went off smoothly, and not one of us will ever know the touch of suspicion. But you are sadly upset. I feared this. That was why I dropped in—to quiet you, if needed, and get you back to normal. Brace yourself, Charles. You do not take enough exercise, I fear. You should walk abroad in the cool of the day. Better still, you should have a saddle horse. I would strongly advise you to ride.'

'Perhaps I will.'

'Begin this very afternoon,' urged Kames warmly. 'That's good advice. But perhaps it will be difficult to get a saddle horse today. Because of our late misfortune, the riding men and the fighting men are all gone.' He opened his watch, glanced at it, and slid from the desk to his feet as he returned the watch to his pocket. With the same movement a revolver shone in his hand, making a double click as he thrust the muzzle against Nash's ear. 'That is the reason, my dear Charles, that you must open your safe,' said Kames kindly. 'The fighting men have all gone north, and I am going south.'

His dear Charles will never be so white in his coffin as he was in that evil dream. 'Ellis! For God's sake!'

'Not at all,' said Ellis. 'For my sake entirely. I had always contemplated this, as a possibility. When Lindauer's cashier told him that our haul was even larger than our highest hopes, I knew the time had come for a bold stroke. I trust, for your own sake ——'

'Ellis! You wouldn't kill me?'

'If you think not, raise your voice,' said Kames savagely. 'If you think not, hesitate. Make one second's delay. Move, Nash! Your life hangs on a hair!'

Nash went to the safe, stumbling, all but falling. He groped at the combination, he swung the great door open.

'Pass that valise out,' said Kames. Nash obeyed. Kames shoved it back with his foot. 'Put your right hand behind you. I'll not have you shooting at me as I leave. Quick, man! Death is at your shoulder!'

Nash thrust his arm back; a handcuff snapped on his wrist. 'Now your left hand behind you. Clear around!'

But as the left hand came back, Kames snapped

the empty cuff on the shank of the long handle of the safe door. Instantly, a second handcuff gripped Nash's left wrist. Kames jerked the loose end back and shackled it, as he had done with the first, on the handle of the safe. He thrust the revolver into a scabbard under his long coat, so that it hung at his left side, butt forward, just in front of the hip socket. He stepped back and picked up the brown valise.

'You can always explain, Charles—in case you should choose to give the alarm. Good-bye!'

Nash fell to his knees as he realized his awful situation. 'They'll kill me,' he whispered with bloodless lips.

'It will be your part to be gone,' said Kames. 'I advised riding, you remember.' He threw open the back door and stepped out into the alley.

Shooting his eyes to right and left, he made for the street. The first two steps were hasty, almost a run. The man was not iron. But with the third step he began to slow down, meaning the next step to fall into the casual, unhurried walk of a mind at peace. He heard a slight noise above him and glanced up.

Aurelio Sais looked over the parapet of the house across the alley, holding a double-barreled shotgun upon him. The muzzle was not ten feet from his head. 'Keep your eyes like that,' said Aurelio without heat or hurry. 'If you look down—if your hands move ever so slightly—that will be all. You are holding the little bag in your right hand. Hold it—oh, so still! That is not wise for a man in such business. You should always keep the gun hand free. I saw the whole play through the window, Mr. Kames. I am surprised at you. To rob is not well, but to break the faith—oh, that is shameless! Think, I beg you, how that unlucky Nash now hears you and sees you—and with how much joy.' His steady eye looked down the barrels without moving, but his voice rose to a great shout:

'Ho-o-o! Hawkins! Munro! Johnny Pardee! *Á mi!*'

On their way to the Nash store, Lindauer, Hawkins and Pardee were midstreet as that wild cry rang out. Hawkins went then to war. It is not too much to say that he removed himself from that place. When Lindauer and the lame Pardee reached the entrance to the alley, Hawkins had already searched Kames for weapons. The brown valise was at his feet, with the Kames revolver beside it; his rifle covered the double traitor. Aurelio laughed down from his wall.

'Johnny,' said Hawkins, a little breathlessly, 'will you take this rifle? I am close to pulling the trigger, and that is what I do not want to do.' He kicked the brown bag viciously. The unshaken man was shaken now, color came and went in his dark face. 'If this play had gone wrong—and me thinking I was so smart! Never again do I peer into the future. Things happen that you don't expect—like this.'

''Enry,' said Johnny Pardee, 'I am beginning to think that Ellis Kames is not reliable. That's what fooled you. Kames ain't dependable.'

'I will come down now,' said Aurelio. 'I observed through the window. He was most unhappy, that Nash, for he must account for that money to his friends, it seems. That *pobrecito!* And now he hears us and is curious as to his future. But if Nash is terrified, this man is crushed and broken. Look, all this time he has not said one word.'

It was true. The cunning man was voiceless now, his crooked tongue had failed him; his face was the face of a fiend. A train whistle came to their ears; the westbound was coming into Target. Kames trembled at the sound. Aurelio joined them as they listened.

'Think!' said Hawkins in a great voice. 'If this clever Kames had gone quietly out the front way, stopping at the counter to have his valise wrapped and tied, he might have walked over to the train and made a clean getaway.' He drew out his knife, he slashed the bag across; he spread the gash apart and looked in. 'That's the money, all right. I was beginning to be afraid Nash had switched the bag on Kames. I'm losing faith in everybody. . . . Take it, Lindauer; I'll not draw a long breath till it's back in the safe. I was near losing it for you. I had the brilliant idea to throw a gun down on the cashier and make him put it back in the safe. That's all off now. I want it to go back, and do it quick. Aurelio, are any of your folks in there?'

'Not one. My *tío*, he is old. And I sent him away, not knowing what might happen here.'

'That's good. Johnny, do you think you can take this shotgun and hold Mr. Kames in Aurelio's house till Aurelio and I come for him?'

'I can try,' said Johnny. 'At least I'll make a reasonable effort to hold him. But if he gets away after I give him both barrels, I can't help it. He'll just have to go. I can't run.'

'This play simplifies matters,' said Hawkins. 'We will have a little more to do. Then Aurelio and I will take Mr. Kames off your hands. We won't let word get out, and if we possibly can, we'll get him out of town without attracting any attention.'

'Why not?' said Aurelio. 'There are few left to see. The railroad men have their own troubles. And if anyone notes us, what is there to see? Three friends, riding out together. No more than that. We can make it a point with Mr. Kames that he shall go quietly. Besides, what can he say? What can he ever say? Take him in, Johnny.'

'Oh, Mr. Hollocher,' said Lindauer, to his distracted cashier, when the three friends had arrived safely in the bank, 'here is that money that was taken a while ago.' He shoved the violated valise through the wicket.

The cashier plunged trembling hands into the bills and lifted them. 'But—but——' he gurgled, with bulging eyes fixed upon Hawkins.

Lindauer laid an affectionate hand upon the suspect's shoulder. 'It was not Mr. Hawkins,' he said, laughing. 'The robber was dressed like him, purposely, so that Hawkins should have the blame. Max, that this bank is not ruined, we owe it to many brave friends, but most of all to this good friend here. And this town, Max, from now on it will be a fit place to live in. And we shall owe it to Mr. Hawkins.'

'Shucks!' said Mr. Hawkins, embarrassed. 'Mr. Max, you want to check up that money. It may not be all there. For all we know, Dave Salt got a chance to shovel a handful of it down in his pants. I wouldn't put it past him.' He turned to Lindauer. 'You spoke of thanking me. If you mean it, let me work this thing out my own way. You could send a few to the pen—Salt and Nash and Kames for sure. For the others, you'd only have my word. Even so, what I know covers only a small part of the gang. Your town is rotten with crooks, all working together. I don't want to send any man to the pen. And I particularly want to manage so that no one gets killed this trip. But if you'll not let it be known for twenty-four hours that you got your money back—if you won't say a word about Kames—in fact, if you won't say nothing to nobody about anything—you leave it to me and I'll throw such a scare into this burg that the last and least will think the devil is clawing at his elbow. You'll not need to clean up. Them that stays in Target will sure have a clean conscience.'

'It is a go,' said Lindauer. . . . 'You hear, Max? . . . You hear, Aurelio?'

'That ain't all, either,' said Hawkins. 'They won't get together again, somewhere else, and do it all over. Somebody tipped the mitt and they'll suspect everybody. If two of these men ever meet in California, one will head for Australia and the other for the North Pole. But I'll have to be boss till sundown today. Is it a go?'

'Surely. But you will not find the bank ungrateful.'

'That's good. You can give me a box of ca'tridges,

then, and collect from the bank. . . . Come on, Mr. Lindauer; you and me and Aurelio have got a couple of short visits to make. Then me and Aurelio'll buy us a small snack of dinner—after which the two of us will take Mr. Kames and proceed to bring the fear of God to Gridiron. We'll want a horse for Kames. Here, let's take Aurelio visiting with us.'

'I declare,' said Lindauer, in the street, 'it seems like Sunday, don't it?'

'It does so. Nobody seen us since I come alive, not even when Aurelio was yelling bloody murder. They're all talking it up, in the saloon.'

They visited the Nash store first. The office door was shut, and customers went about the store. Walter, the clerk, was busy and cheerful. It was evident that Nash had not seen fit to give the alarm. In his private mind, Mr. Hawkins felt confident that Nash was now on his travels; a guess that lacked something to fit the fact. Nash had seen Kames taken, had heard every word spoken in the alley. He knew that his own guilt was established beyond question, and his only hope was for mercy; and he now awaited the next turn of the wheel with what patience he could muster, not uncomforted by recent events in the alley.

It was Hawkins who opened the office door. His

jaw dropped when he saw that Nash was shackled to his own safe. He pointed, voiceless; color swept his face as he turned to Lindauer and Aurelio.

'I told him this morning not to do that!' said Hawkins, and bit his lip with vexation. 'Here I preached up as far as fourthly to you fellows, over in the bank, just to give Nash time to make his get-away—and behold you, he hasn't budged.'

Nash turned imploring eyes on the banker. 'You'll help me get loose, Hermie?' he faltered. 'For the sake of old times?'

But Lindauer, whose contempt had wasted no word on Kames, flamed now to anger. His friendship with Nash was a thing long past, but he felt betrayed. He spread out his hands.

'How are we to know you wanted loose? It is your place and you might run it to suit yourself. If you choose to make such arrangements, why should I interfere? If you want loose you should attend to it. Nobody will stop you. I'll sell your clerk a file for cash. I bid you good day.'

'But, Hermie, we are making one big mistake,' said Aurelio when they reached the street once more.

'Yes. We should send these thugs to the pen for life,' said Hermie, wiping his wrist across his brow.

'Not that. If all was known that I know,' said

Aurelio, 'one who would now be serving time would be Aurelio Sais. I know just how Mr. Hawkins feels. Also, his way will be best for us. Only the leaders were concerned in robbing your bank. If we send them up, the main army would still be with us. The other way, fear will be at their backs. Fear of the unknown. The Gridiron gang is a smashed egg, and all the king's horses and all the king's men can never get it together again. But that was not what I meant. Hawkins is supposed to have been Bill Doolin, and to have robbed your bank—and it is only good luck that somebody has not taken a shot at him already. Don't you think it would be pleasant if you would go over to the Jim Gem saloon and make oration? You don't have to explain. Tell them that it was impossible for Hawkins to have robbed your bank, because he was closeted with you at the time of the robbery.'

'Sure! We have been taking chances.' He started to go, but the Mexican caught at his sleeve. 'Another thing, *amigo*. You're overlooking one bet.' Aurelio's speech was cold and precise as a usual thing, smacking of the schools. But now, in his anxiety not to give offense to his friend, he became almost colloquial. 'You want to clean up Target, Hermie? Well, there is one thing you can do that will be a big help. Make your store larger—or your hotel. The Holland House hasn't near enough bedrooms. Why don't you make your saloon into bedrooms?'

'But—but it is not my saloon. I just rent it to Jim,' said Lindauer, flushing. 'The guests want their liquor, and my customers in the store. I like a little drink myself.'

'I like a little drink, too. That's not the question. Jim's Gem makes the headquarters of crime under your roof. Kick him out. He can find other places. You know very well that when you want to hire a man to shoot someone in the back, you never mention the matter to a man that's working. You go straight to the saloon. Don't you?'

'Always. I remember now,' admitted Lindauer fretfully. He flapped his hands wingwise. 'All righd, all righd—don't sing no hymns! Have it your own way. I make me a fine big hotel and lose money by it.' He turned back to Lindauer Place, grumbling and muttering, still winging his way.

Judge Humphries was slipping a pan of sourdough biscuit into the oven when Aurelio knocked. He came to the door wiping his hands, a smile of welcome spreading to greet Aurelio; a smile which became fixed and frozen as he saw who stood beyond.

Hawkins sniffed. 'Lord 'a' mercy, is that wool I smell burning? Judge, have you went and burned up that old black hat? Why, you old skeesicks, I wanted that hat for Exhibit A. . . . Never mind, I'll use this one of mine. The grateful bank will just nicely have to buy me a new one, 'cause I need this for a special purpose, and my money is low, and I'm taking the road right sho'tly. . . . Judge, I'm taking that old saddle and bridle, out behind. Kames wants it. Be around and get it after a bit. Good-bye, Judge! C'mon, 'Relio. Don't you see the judge wants to think it over?'

A modest sign upon the wall near the judge's front door caught his eye. It was this notice to the world:

FRANCIS TRUESDALE HUMPHRIES
Justice of the Peace
Notary Public
Land Laws
Location Notices
Blanks of All Kinds

Hawkins paused and considered this sign long and earnestly. 'You got a pencil, Aurelio?' he said at last. 'Well, wish you'd write a little note on this sign for me.'

'Ready,' said Aurelio, and wrote there as dictated:

Gone to Europe. May not be back till sundown.

CHAPTER XI

WHEN THE TIME CAME for the posse to split and fan, there was argument, even as foreseen by Hawkins on the housetop. Marshal Yewell did not want Farr, and said as much with point and vigor; while Farr would hear of no other decision. Also, Erie Patterson inclined strongly to go with his own men. It required all the firmness and persuasion that Lewis could bring to bear to make the arrangement according to his wish. Once over the hill to Staircase, he pointed out, the marshal could pick up more men. As to old Elmer, he was only exercising a perverse and misbegotten sense of humor. Elmer would be a good man in a pinch. He asked Erie to recall that cowboys had never functioned for two masters, and never would. They would work for the foreman or they would work for the owner, but the world never went well when both were on the job.

'You side us, Erie, and let Curly rod your peelers,' said the jovial Lewis. 'You can help to keep an eye on old Elmer, so the marshal's nerves can sorter quiet down.'

Moreover, as to the aid of Frank John, the marshal showed a singular lack of enthusiasm; shrugging his wide shoulders and wrinkling his aristocratic Roman nose. Thus in disfavor, Farr and Frank John tagged along in the blistering heat, far behind to escape the dust; and to my first, my second imparted much information about my third, fourth and fifth; in fact, about Gridiron as a whole, with a spirited résumé of all that Farr had missed during his brief imprisonment.

They rode swiftly. That is to say—in order that there shall be no misunderstanding in this matter—the trot they used for distance was a long, steady, reaching trot. They stood up in their stirrups, leaning forward, steady on the bit. This forced-draft gait was good for six miles an hour; which means many miles from sun to sun, as may be verified with pencil and paper if you are of a mathematical turn. Or, it may be verified by riding. In the latter case you will observe that the long, hard trot will take you, in the time mentioned, just twice as far as the same horse can carry you at the gay gallop—with the further advantage that you would still have a live horse the next morning. It was expressly provided in the Treaty of Guadalupe-Hidalgo that no posse should gallop except when the fugitive was actually visible, and then only when the prisoner was not only in sight, but also out of gunshot. It is believed that moving pictures have changed all this. But they have never told the horses.

Eighteen miles brought them to one o'clock and the foothills. Erie spoke of the good lunch at his saddle horn, and the marshal spoke of Gib Newell's ranch at Clingstone, just over the divide and eight miles farther on—not trotting miles but climbing miles. Once more Lewis overruled them:

'Up that second little side canyon on the left-hand side, just beyond the second bend, is a place we ought to look,' said he. 'The old Red Sleeve mine. Natural hide-out, little spring, lookout and back stairs—everything. Place where a man could hide a year and never be found. Many's the time I've thought about it, studyin' what I'd do if I had spunk enough. Why not go make a look-see there? If we don't find no trace of our bold bandit, we can eat our lunch and then toddle along up to Clingstone.'

'Red Sleeve?' echoed Erie. 'Why, I thought that was the old Mangas Mine.'

'Same thing. Red Sleeve is Mangas Colorado in English. Low-grade copper. No good. Bless my soul and body! Near twenty years since I was up there, workin' for Bige Witherspoon. Man, that's a long time ago! Grant was President, the Frenchies was fighting Bismarck, and I had a girl in Santa

Rita, 'n' one night, as I was comin' home, I stumbled over a star. This was a fine country then.'

Avoiding discussion, he waved his hand to hurry up the laggards, and turned from the road. His mind thus made up, the marshal soon took the lead, quite unsuspicious of the fact that his ways were gently guided. The rear guard closed up briskly and rejoined the others at the first bend of the canyon.

There was a short box, then another sharp bend. The canyon opened to a natural amphitheater, gracious and wide, parked with spicy cedar and spicy juniper. Beyond was a low, rolling divide, wavy and meandering, topped on the very crest by a spiny dike; like nothing so much as the woodcuts of the Chinese wall in the back of the geography book. And in that dike there was a gap, and in that gap there was a house, sagging and weather-gray; and near that house there sprawled an old mining dump, melting into the hill, reclaimed now by grass and wild poppies and firefly bush; and on that dump there was a windlass; exactly like a riddle.

The answer was soon found. There was no track of horse or man; the ghastly house was a skull, with eyeless sockets where windows had been, and an open door between; bleached and gray, the windlass posts stood out against the sky line, spectral and startling. Unurged, curious, the marshal led the way, sidelong against the slope. Patterson was next. Because, no man has lived who could resist the impulse to look down a well or a shaft. It is compulsory.

Lewis and Farr pulled their rifles from the scabbards. Frank John wished that he hadn't come and was glad he did. The leaders left their horses at the edge of the dump and went directly to the shaft, without once looking back. Long planks covered it, with bowlders to hold them down. They rolled away the smallest bowlder, levered the plank aside and knelt to peer down the shaft. Lewis made a long arm and jerked Yewell's gun from the scabbard at his hip. Farr would have done as much for Patterson. But Erie Patterson heard, or saw, or sensed—himself could not tell you how. With an inch to spare, with half a fraction of some small part of a second, his body dived forward from that crouching position on hands and knees, lunged like a sword thrust, twisting in the air as he plunged. He fell on his back across the planking, his clutching hand all but touching his gun, but with the gun partly under him as he had fallen. He held his hand there, unmoving, and looked up with steady, unfearing eyes.

'I'll never rot in the pen!' said Erie Patterson. 'You'll get me, of course. But when one foot moves this way I go for my gun.'

Farr's rifle covered him, Farr's foot was almost touching his, but the clear eyes did not waver, and there was no shadow in them. The man was beautiful. Lewis still held his rifle thwartwise in his left hand; his right hand held the marshal's revolver trained upon Patterson's ribs, all but touching them. The marshal made no observation. The marshal was sickly green and frozen where he knelt. Frank John was trying to breathe.

'You fool, I've got a bead on your gizzard!' cried Farr.

'And I've got my eye on your belt buckle,' said Patterson, with an even voice. 'It's a bad draw, but the longer you talk the better my chances. I hit my crazy bone when I did a flop. Nasty jar, but it's better now. And I've arched my hip enough to let my gun loose. Come on, I'm ready. I've lived free, and I'll die that way!'

'I get your point, Erie,' said Pres approvingly. 'But you're all wrong. Just hold your horses, will you? Nobody wants to put you in the pen.'

'No, nor I won't hang, either,' said Erie. There was no bravado in his defiance. 'You can never bury me cheaper, and I'll take company with me. You may hang Erie Patterson's dead body, but you'll never hang me.'

'Why, Erie!' said Farr. 'Such an idea never entered my head.'

'Liar!'

'I'm not moving till we get the news into your thick skull,' said Farr patiently. 'Don't you move, either. If I was to kill you, you might never get over it.'

'Farr's telling you true,' said Pres Lewis. 'This isn't the law. This is a private enterprise—one of them Italian vendettas, like Troy Ware's got on his new house.'

'I don't believe any such a thing. What have I ever done to you?'

'You don't understand, son. This here little feud has got nothing to do with the past. It's all in the future. You ain't never goin' to forgive me. I feel it in my bones. No, sir, in all the years to come, you're always goin' to feel a grudge against old Pres. And you can have long years to get even, if you'll just be reasonable and unbuckle that belt with your left hand, and then get up, right hand first, leaving your gun lay. Then we can talk it over. You're just so heady, we can't talk good while you've got that gun handy. If you had the brains God gives a grasshopper, you'd know that we never meant to kill you. If we did, why are you living along all over the shop?'

Patterson considered this at some length. 'Oh, I believe that much of it,' he conceded. 'You don't want to kill me, but you want my gun. You don't get it. That gun stands between me and the pen.'

'No such thing,' said Farr. 'I swan, Erie, I'm getting out of patience with you. You deserve the pen, of course. Who don't? But it was set down beforehand that nobody was to go to the pen this trip. And nobody to get killed, if it could be managed convenient.'

'What are you driving at then, you speckle-faced maniac?'

'I don't rightly know all the ins and outs of it myself, me being in jail,' said the maniac, pleasantly enough, but with a wary eye upon his opponent's gizzard. 'It seems the Almighty sent His pussonal representative to look over this neck of the woods, near as I can make out. Sort of inspector like—and he has an idee you're the lost Charlie Ross. I think he is the Angel Gabriel, maybe, from all I hear. What he says goes, anyhow, just like he was the doctor. And from what Frank John tells me, back there in the dust, Gabe is a heap more tender-hearted than ever I gave him credit for. "Gosh, I don't want nobody sent to no pen," says Gabe. "They might not be satisfied there. I know I wouldn't be." '

'It wasn't Gabriel,' said Pres. 'It was Abijah K. Witherspoon. And what Farr says is true. The last words Bige said to me: "Woodman, whatever you do," he says, "you spare that tree, if it's anyways possible." And he ain't going to be any too well pleased, either, me setting your mind at ease, like this. His idea was that you'd be speculating and worrying about your past life, and how much of it had leaked out—and here I do believe you're planning along for the future right now. It's discouraging, that's what it is,' said Lewis. 'But Bige would have done the same, if he'd been here. He didn't know you had so much internal economy. How could he? Well, you never can tell till you try. But I'm real pleased with you, Erie. I am so. Now you be reasonable. Nobody's asking you to give up your gun. You just get up and go away and leave your gun where it is.'

'Indeed, Mr. Patterson, I heard them agree that no one was to be imprisoned, or even arrested,' said Frank John, speaking for the first time. 'Word of honor,' he added earnestly. 'Why should a boy, a perfect stranger, lie to you, perjure himself about it?'

Patterson turned this idea over in his mind. 'Huh! Something in that too. All right, then. My back itches, anyhow.' He raised his right hand high, unbuckled his belt, and got up, holding to the windlass post; he rubbed his right elbow, gingerly. 'That elbow's still tingling,' he said. 'That was hard luck, me doing that. Put me plumb out of business.'

'There, Frank John; I told you we needed you,' said Pres. 'Nothing like a good old Maryland name to make a little party respectable. Erie didn't half believe us—but just a word from you, and everything was lovely. Now, Frank John, you pick up these extra guns and tote 'em over by the horses. If anybody starts to come that way, you flip a pebble at 'em. . . . Yewell, get up and stand over there by Erie, so Elmer can keep an eye on both of you.' He began moving the bowlders from the rotting planks. 'Come to think of it, I camped here a spell, only last year, deer hunting. The windlass is over in the old house. We'll bring the windlass over and take our saddle ropes——'

'Like hell!' said Erie, and plunged over the steep dump. But Frank John started with him, two steps and a long jump, and landed on Patterson's shoulders while both were in the air. They rolled together in rolling stones and dust, they struggled to their knees at the foot of the dump, bruised, bleeding, breathless from the fall. Lewis was just behind; the two together grappled with this dauntless enemy and brought him down, struggling manfully, wordless. Farr herded the marshal to the horses, before his rifle, took down a saddle rope; he brought marshal and rope to the writhing huddle below; they bound Patterson hand and foot, helpless, but still defiant.

'Liar!' said Erie. His eyes were blazing.

'I shall expect a written apology for that before the week is out,' replied Lewis, with great dignity. 'Just as soon as you are safe on the bounding billow, you drop me a post card. But it's just as well. If you think, for a day or two, that you're going to the pen, that will be next best to actually going there. We are going to send down grub and water to you—with you, rather. Make you all nice and comfy. You can be thinking it over. You'll have lots of time. There's a short tunnel, running north from the bottom of the shaft. That's the place I was telling you about—where a man could hide. Shaft is a hundred feet deep, even. Ten assessment works. Three saddle ropes will just nicely make it. Come on, marshal. We'll let you down first. You stay here, Erie.'

'You go to hell!' said Erie.

Taking Yewell with them, they brought the windlass from the deserted house, rigged it on the posts and turned it till the three saddle ropes were tied together and neatly wound to the end, leaving only a loop for the marshal's foot. Lewis brought from his saddle bags a folded newspaper and a candle. 'I've thought of everything, Yewell,' he said cheerfully. He lit the newspaper and dropped it down the shaft. 'That's to test it out for foul air,' he explained. 'It burns all right, so that part is over. I'd hate to have you poisoned. And the candle, that's because rattlesnakes fall in sometimes, or skunks. That'll give you light to kill 'em by, if so be you find any. You take your canteens and lunch, this trip. Then we'll send Erie down to you and you can untie him.' In spite of frantic prayers and entreaties, they forced Yewell to put foot and hand to the rope, and lowered away. Canteens and lunch were draped over his shoulders.

'I hope that rope don't break on you, Jim,' said Farr kindly, as the marshal's head disappeared in the shaft. 'Purty good rope, though. I guess it will hold you.'

The calculation was exact. When the rope went slack only a yard remained on the windlass. 'All right below?' said Lewis. 'Take your foot out. Now you look for snakes while we get Erie.'

The three of them carried Erie, who enlivened the short journey by his opinions, some of which were novel and unexpected. All were new to Frank John.

They tied the windlass rope to Erie's bonds

securely. 'Matches? Tobacco?' said Pres, patting Erie's pockets. 'We can spare you another sack. . . . No? All right then. We got to send you down tied, Erie. If we didn't I do believe you'd let go, just out of spite. You suhtenly are the beatin'est man!'

Erie expressed his thanks for this compliment in suitable terms. They lowered away then. But when a few feet of rope had been paid out Pres stopped the windlass. 'I declare, Erie, I forgot to ask you for the key to that valise!' he said. . . . 'Elmer, we'll have to pull this bundle up again.'

'Oh, we can cut the valise open,' said Elmer. 'I don't want to work this windlass all day. I want to eat. I'm all hot and flustered. . . . Frank John, you can be bringing the lunch and canteens over here.'

The bundle made no reply, probably because its thoughts were running on keys and valises. They lowered it to the bottom and Yewell untied it from the windlass rope. They did not wind the windlass up this time, but pulled the rope up hand over hand, untied it and coiled it neatly to three blameless saddle ropes again.

Lewis sat with his legs hanging in the shaft, held a canteen between his legs, pulled the cork and gazed mildly at hill and sky. ' "It is a far, far better thing I do now than I have ever done before," ' he murmured mistily.

'Huh?' said Elmer. But Frank John, something overwrought and strained of spirit, strangled in his water drinking. He had not yet learned the management of a canteen.

They ate their lunch to the last crumb, dropping its wrappings into the shaft. Then Pres sighed comfortably, took out a plug of tobacco, turned it critically, this way and that, worried off a propitious corner, and gazed down at the spark of light that was the candle.

'Erie,' he called down, 'are you there?'

Erie indicated that he was there. Pres listened admiringly, and waited for a strategic moment.

'What do you want us to do with your horses?' Pres inquired, as Erie paused for breath. 'And your guns?'

Erie told him what he might do with the horses and the guns. A drowsy silence followed. Elmer lit his pipe. Then Pres spoke to the shaft again:

'It's sure blazing hot up here, fellows. Reg'lar old scorcher. Thunder-heads peeping up above the hills. I betcha we're going to have a rain. If it does, you boys had better go in the tunnel, so's to keep dry.'

The shaft made no answer.

'Erie, are you still down there? Anything we can

send you out from town? Deck of cards, or a bottle? Mail? Newspapers?'

Erie replied, in effect, that he wanted for nothing; and blew out the candle.

'Oh, all right, if that's the way you feel about it. But we'll send you some more grub and water anyway—tomorrow, or maybe next day. Erie, you don't know any good songs, do you? Mrs. Lofty? Beautiful Mabel Clare?' He cleared his throat and sang huskily, with trembling tenderness:

In the gloaming, oh, my darling,
Think not bitter-lee of me!

'Hey? What's that?' Looking down, Lewis could no longer see those moving shadows in the dusk below. The other members of the posse had retired to the privacy of their tunnel. It was plain that they lacked artistic feeling.

Lewis rose up and squinted at the sun. 'Oh, well, if you don't want to be friendly we'll go on in to Target.'

CHAPTER XII

HAWKINS AND AURELIO SAIS made an early dinner, well before midday, through courtesy of the management. They strolled to the feed corral. The new horse, sent to substitute for the vanished Smoky, was a stockingfoot sorrel, and Hawkins greeted him at once as Mittens, though without previous acquaintance.

'He looks like that kind of a horse,' said 'Enry, none too well pleased. ' "Two white feet, buy him; three white feet, try him," ' he quoted. 'This varmint has got four white feet. Oh, well! Mr. Gray, Pres Lewis left this horse here, and I haven't any more papers than a road lizard. What with the wild excitement and all, Lewis plumb forgot.'

'Sais says you're to take him. That's good.'

'And we want another for the day,' said Aurelio. 'No saddle. Mr. Hawkins has another saddle.'

'A slow horse, named Terrapin,' amended Hawkins. 'We want a slow horse, most particular. . . . Aurelio, would you mind callin' me 'Enry? Mr.

Hawkins seems so stiff and formal, and I'm tired of Hawkins, anyway. Bill is such a common name—awful common. But 'Enry sounds friendly. You call me 'Enry, and I'll call you 'Eadlight.'

Aurelio laughed, pushing back his high-crowned and tomato-colored Mexican hat to show a mop of flaming hair. 'Make it Goldie,' he suggested. 'That's my name in English. And my gray horse is Plata. Silver and gold.'

They led Terrapin into the alley behind the Humphries' horse box, to saddle him with the sorry rig they found there. They found no saddle blanket, so they went into the house to take one from the judge's bed. The judge was not within. A scorchy smell filled the kitchen. Goldie opened the oven. The biscuits were burned. They passed into the front room. The door was open. A watchful and bright-eyed tortoise-shell cat curled on the cushion of the rocking-chair, and purred under Goldie's hand. A book lay open on the table, face down to hold the place; Aurelio spread out his hands. '*Se fué!*' he said solemnly. ''Enry, the judge is gone.'

'Just as well,' said 'Enry. 'He was a purty old man and he couldn't stand the razzle-dazzle we're dealing. Goldie, Old Man Lindauer says you're due to be sheriff, soon as they can get his resignation to

Davis. I guess that includes the custody of the cat. That cat's going to be right lonesome. Bring him along. His name is Grayback.'

They saddled Terrapin, and behind the saddle they tied a black hat, a small and slashed valise and a meal sack; they walked down the alley, leading the horses. Goldie carried the cat, making small reassuring noises in golden Spanish; he knocked at his *tío*'s door.

'We come for Kames,' he stated simply, as Johnny Pardee opened to him.

'Moses in the bulrushes!' said Johnny. 'I thought you was never coming. What in time have you been doing?'

'You run on and peddle your papers, Johnny. Grub pile ready, and what you don't know won't hurt you. Mr. Kames and Goldie and me are going to take a little ride,' said 'Enry. 'It may be the last ride we will ever take together,' he added, not without emotion.

Kames shrieked: 'Johnny, he means to murder me! Don't let them take me; come with them if they take me. They don't intend to take me to jail. Come with me, for God's sake.'

'I got to go to dinner,' said Johnny. 'Get Nash to go with you.'

'Nash's place is closed,' said 'Enry. 'I saw that

poor little clerk's face through the window. Scared stiff, he was. 'D-by, buster!'

'Good-bye? Why, 'Enry, you'll be back?'

'After what's going to happen to Kames? Not likely. Folks are mighty suspicious of these accidents, like this. Take keer of yourself, kid. Watch your cinches!'

Aurelio took Kames by the arm and towed him out into the alley. 'You remember Ouray, Kames? His name is Terrapin now. And you know Ouray is not what you might call a fast horse. All right, then. We'll allow you to keep with us till we get out of town. Then you ride ahead, out of earshot. You poison the air. When you come to a fork in the road, you look back. I'll motion to you which way to go. Then you can use your own judgment. It would be better for you to take the way I show you. If you meet anyone coming, give 'em the road—and ride wide. Not a word out of you, good or bad, to anyone. You are practically extinct.'

'Aurelio, what are you going to do with me? Oh, have pity! What are you going to do?' A thin scream, like an animal's, burst from Kames' quivering lips. In his abject terror the coward buckled and fell, and clasped his hands together, groveling in the sand, where Goldie surveyed him with loathing and disgust.

'Get up, you white-livered hound!' he said. 'Get on that horse. Don't open your filthy mouth again. What will we do? Not what you are afraid of; and nothing that you'll ever guess. Ride!' As the lawyer mounted, his eye fell, for the first time, on the evidence behind the saddle, and he lacked but little of a stroke.

'That meal sack isn't really the same one,' said 'Enry. 'I meant to get the one Dave had, but when I saw how you had fixed up Nash, I was so flabbergasted I forgot. You might have knocked me down with a crowbar. You mustn't mind what Sais says. That's just his way. He's so blamed upright. You've got a right to be scared.'

They crossed the railroad beyond the stockyards, and circled back to Staircase road, leaving the Carmody herd on the left. No need to make inquiries, said 'Enry; if Pres Lewis had failed to make up his party as planned, he, 'Enry, would have had word of it. Far to the left, a dust cloud on the plain, coming down from San Lorenzo; a dust that was, by all the doctrines of chance and probability, Charlie Bird returning with the recovered herd. 'Enry wondered if Charlie Bird had found the thief; and if so, was it a case of kill or capture? Kames rode on before, twenty yards, thirty; a drooped and dejected wreck of a man, he who had been so jaunty and so arrogant, so scornful of the humble and the poor.

High above them and far away, black spots wove dimly through the dark bushes along the winding road. A glitter of light on metal, figures that shaped and grew, became men and horses, became three men and five horses, became a slender man, a blocky man, a short man. Aurelio drew rein where a soapweed clump made shade, for the sun was hot and hot. He waved the dismal Kames from the road, waved him to circle back, keeping his distance; stopped him at last where he could be well watched. Goldie sat under a soapweed then, and held his rifle across his knees.

'Bless my soul, if it isn't the gifted 'Enry and little Goldilocks!' said Pres. 'But who is that out yonder? Isn't that neighbor Kames?'

'Light down, light down. That is what was Kames. But how about you? Whatever has happened to our wandering boy today?'

'Frank John,' said Elmer, 'has been to war. Don't he look it?'

He looked it. The man all tattered and torn had never a shirt so split and fluttering. His hands looked like a cat fight, his face was raked across where he had used it for a sled runner on the loose rock of the Mangas dump, an ear lopped askew for lack of needed repairs, one eye was puffed and swollen, beautifully black; and no swashbuckler of all time had ever borne himself so proudly, not even the storied hero who could strut while sitting down.

'He did that planting Patterson, as per agreement,' said Lewis, paternally proud. 'I must tell you about Patterson. Not now, though. Kames first. What has Kames been and gone and done now?'

'You'd never guess. Get down, all of you, and I'll tell you about Kames.'

'Oh and ah,' said Elmer politely, in a small, mouse voice. He stifled a yawn with three slender fingers. 'If that is all—if you're quite sure that is all—why, you got no more use for me, and I'll go on about my business. You fellows can all go back to Mangas mine together, or you can all go back to town together, or you can stay right here and swap stories. I don't care. I'm going to cut across to the Ladder Line Camp and see if I can't persuade Albert Garst to work for me. You boys just prattle away.' He swung into the saddle, but paused for a moment. 'It's going to be right queer, though, when the sheriff gets back. Nobody owning Erie's cattle or Nash's store. Property squandering around loose, right and left. Marshal gone, judge gone. And nobody saying a word. I declare, that's goin' to be real shivery and scaresome.'

'Enry wore a shamefaced look. 'I think maybe the sheriff won't come back,' he said, much embarrassed. 'I think possibly that jailer or somebody might slip out and put a bug in the sheriff's ear. In fact, I know he will. Weak-minded of me, I know. But I keep thinking about him standing up for the Carmody woman and the Carmody kids. Dave Salt, he's just a tool and a cat's-paw. But that dumb, pot-bellied old sheriff is some part of a man, even yet.'

'I know,' said Pres soberly. 'Elmer and me and the youngster, we hog-tied a real man today, and let him down that shaft like a calf in a crate. . . . What makes 'em go bad, 'Enry? Why can't they be straight?'

'Enry made a wry face and shook his head. 'Well, there's no use of everybody looking at me for information,' said Elmer with decision. 'Because I'm done and gone. This conversation is getting entirely too personal to suit me.' He flicked his quirt and set out on his promised visit.

'Frank John is tired,' said Pres. 'Goldie, you go back to town with him, and me and 'Enry will escort the wearisome Kames out to the mine and drop him in. We want one of your saddle ropes, though. Kames hasn't got any on his saddle.'

Clouds hurried across the sky when they came to the dump of that old mine, and the sun was nearing the hills. They ordered the outcast to dismount. Kames thought his hour had come; knew it when he saw his relentless guards take from his saddle all the hateful baggage at which he had shuddered through those dreadful hours. Why should they do that, except they meant killing? They would leave that damning evidence with his body.

Pres Lewis leaned on the windlass and shouted down the shaft: 'Hoo-o! You down there yet? . . . This is Lewis. You remember me—Pres Lewis? Sending some stuff down. Get back in your tunnel; I'm going to drop it.' The meal sack fluttered down the shaft. He heard a smothered oath from below. After an interval, to allow for reflection, he dropped down that rolled black hat and the brown bag.

'That will give them something to study about,' said Hawkins. Kames' heart leaped. It was not death, then. They rigged the rope to the windlass, and Kames put his foot in the loop willingly enough. To live—only to live!

'You explain to them, Mr. Kames,' said Pres

kindly. They lowered him to the bottom and rode away; they left the rope there, hanging in the shaft.

'How long do you think it'll take them to climb that rope?' said 'Enry as they turned the first bend.

'No time at all. I betcha Erie is halfway up now—unless he wanted to hear the explanations first. I would sure admire to hear what kind of a tale Kames puts up. I don't think it will be so good. He doesn't seem quite up to the mark today—Kames. What will they think? What will they say? What will they do?'

'Hoof it to the nearest Ladder well, get horses and scatter. And to the day of their death, not one will ever know why he wasn't killed or jugged.'

'Well, how about it, 'Enry? Do we go to town or ease over to Clingstone for the night? It's about eight miles to Clingstone, and getting late.'

They were on the main road now, and the smoke of Target's engines lay far below them. 'Enry stretched out his hand.

'Lewis, there's the only place in the world that thinks well of me.' His mouth twisted to a crooked smile. 'So I'm moving on before they change their minds. You go on to Clingstone. I'll mosey over to that line camp Farr was heading for, if I can find it, and pull out soon in the morning. So this is *ádios*. Take keer of yo'self.'

Spare mount

Courtesy Ruth Koerner Oliver

'I guess not,' said Pres. 'You might run up against some of the Ladder boys, and you want someone to tell 'em it was all a mistake. I'll side you.'

'Enry grinned. 'I'd just about forgot they was looking for me,' he admitted. 'Had a lot on my mind today, and not overmuch sleep last night. Besides, I might not find the camp at night. Been there, but it was from the other side, and daytime. Well, thank you kindly, Mr. Pres. This is right clever of you. Is it far?'

'All of that. There's a short cut through the hills, for them that knows it. Let me lead that horse a spell, 'Enry. If he keeps on holding back I'll ride him myself and lead mine. You roll you a smoke and look pleasant. Night is right on us. Soon be time for taps.' He threw up his head and sang, and echoes brought the slow words back to him:

Go to sleep. Day is gone. Night is on!

'Gosh, I'm tired,' said 'Enry. 'These jugglers, that keep three balls in the air, and a plate and a glass of water, a butcher knife and a canary bird—do you suppose they ever get dizzy, so they can't stop? I feel like that.'

'I get you. Especially about the bird. Erie Patterson isn't yellow, but he certainly is a bird! I guess I won't forget Erie—not ever. What a waste!'

'I seen things today I ain't goin' to forget for quite a spell, either. Queerest of all was that empty house and them burned biscuits, teakettle singing away on the stove, and the cat a-waiting. That's a nice cat. You tell Goldie I said for him to be good to that cat. And then Lindauer, when he agreed to ditch the Gem. Sawin' the air with his little fat arms, and the sun beatin' down on his shiny bald head. 'All righd, all righd—don't sing no hymns!' he says, fanning his head. Funny to think that'll be the last I'll ever see him.'

The way grew wide here, crossing a walled valley, and the two rode side by side. Clouds drifted low over Gridiron; close above them the rose glow of sunset fell over the broken battlements of Horse-Thief Hill.

'Now I've done it again!' announced 'Enry. 'Come away without paying my bill at the hotel, and left my things there. You tell Old Man Lindauer to pay the bill and charge it to the bank; and you can keep the things, if you want 'em, or burn them. Just some duds. . . . But there was one thing—a little tintype. Oh, well!'

Pres said, 'Drop me a post card when you get time, and give me some friend's address. I'll send the picture to your friend and you can get it later. It will not be traced.'

'Enry rode on in silence for a space. Then he lifted quiet eyes. 'Did you know all the time who I was?' he asked.

'Not till last night. Not till you said the marshal was lying to you.'

'Enry ridged his forehead in puzzlement. Then he shrugged. 'I'm tired, I guess. How was it?'

'Young Frank John put his finger on the place when he said you must have some extraordinary motive to make you act the silly way you did. You said it was because you knew the marshal was lying to you, and that there was no guesswork about it. But what the marshal said might have been perfectly true, for all you had any chance to know—all except just one thing. He told you that Bill Doolin and Carmody were old friends. And you had already told us that you had never seen Carmody before—when you sent me out with the letter. And you sent the letter to Charlie Bird; not to Carmody. That's all.'

'Enry nodded. 'I didn't want to see Charlie. I liked Charlie when we was boys.' There was a long pause. 'And Charlie liked me—then.' He rode on in silence. Lewis took the lead as the swift twilight dimmed. They climbed athwart a high hillside and a smother of mist was all about; the black void of night rushed upon them. Shod feet struck fire from the flinty hill. They rounded a shoulder to a steep descent, and came to an open ridge below the fog.

'This is the home stretch,' said Lewis. 'One long straight ridge to the Line Camp, couple or three miles yet.' He checked his horse and waited until the other drew alongside. ''Enry,' said Lewis earnestly, 'why not stay here and play out the string? You've got good friends here. Make your play.'

'No go. It is soon or late with me. This is my bed, like I made it.'

'Target thinks well of you, 'Enry.'

'Even that much I did not come by honestly,' said the other bitterly. 'Lewis, I come to look that bank over myself. Only that I got a down on that gang— You see how it is. Can I build on such a foundation as that?'

'Well, you wouldn't be deceiving me, anyhow,' urged Pres. 'Why not try Jim River? I can make Jim River a sanctuary. You and me, 'Enry, we'd make quite a pair.'

'I'd only drag you down with me. No go. Don't waste your time on me,' said 'Enry. 'I'll quit you here, I think. I know my way now and I guess I'll move on till morning. Couldn't sleep and I don't feel like talking, down at the camp.'

The black and enormous night was about them

as they parted on that bleak and shrill hillside. 'There is only one thing you can do for me,' said 'Enry steadily. 'Target is the one place on earth that will remember me kindly. Let it be Hawkins they remember. Let them wonder what ever did become of Hawkins, and speak kindly of him by campfires. Good-bye.'

'I'm no great shakes myself,' said Lewis, and his voice was warm in the night. 'Such as I am, I wish you well. And I give you Merve Woody's toast:

Here's at ye, and here's to'ard ye;
If we'd never seed ye, we'd a-never knowed ye!

'So long, friend. Take keer of yourself!'

There were no lights in the line-camp house, no sound of horses from the sheds. Pres opened the door and struck a match. He saw an overturned table and broken dishes all about. A lamp lay by the door, and shattered glass beyond. He picked up the lamp and shook it. There was some oil left in it yet, so he lit it with a second match. When the flame burned clear, he raised the lamp high and looked about. The room was littered with broken chairs and crockery, boxes, tinware, trampled towels and torn clothes. The table was splintered, the stove was upset and ashes lay along the floor amid the crushed and battered pipe and ruined stoveware. There was no bedding in the broken bunk. Pres shook his head sadly.

'Old Elmer,' he said, 'has no tact.'